MOTH GIRLS

MOTH GIRLS

Anne Cassidy

HOT
KEY
BOOKS

First published in Great Britain in 2016 by Hot Key Books
Northburgh House, 10 Northburgh Street, London EC1V 0AT

A CIP catalogue record for this book is available from the British Library.

ISBN:978-1-4714-0511-2

1

This book is typeset in 10.5 Berling LT Std using Atomik ePublisher

Printed and bound by Clays Ltd, St Ives Plc

www.hotkeybooks.com

Hot Key Books is part of the Bonnier Publishing Group
www.bonnierpublishing.com

To my sister Sam Morey

Before the Moth Girls were dead they were best friends.

PART ONE: The Present

Mandy

One

The day before the house on Princess Street was due to be demolished, Mandy Crystal stood by the wire fence, looking through it. She stared hungrily, her fingers tugging on a pendant that was hanging from her neck. The windows and front door of the house had been removed and she could glimpse into the shady interior. It wasn't the first time she had looked through the windows of this house. The inside had been dark and gloomy even then, when someone had been living in it.

It had been mostly empty since the killing.

The building itself, the bricks and mortar, looked solid, as if it could stand for a hundred more years. Tomorrow, though, it would be flattened. A block of apartments would replace the house and life would go on as though nothing bad had ever happened there.

Mandy's bag was weighing heavily on her shoulder so she allowed it to slip down her arm onto the ground. On the pavement the leaves scuttled around her feet. She trod on some and felt them crackle with dryness. It was getting dark and the sky looked bruised. The autumn sun had slipped away, leaving streaks of pink in its wake.

Mandy sighed and went to leave but something caught her eye. She turned, and saw two discs of red floating in the air, near the roof. She peered at them more closely and saw brilliant red circles undulating one way and then the other.

It was a pair of red helium balloons tied together with ribbon. She looked round, but there was no one nearby. She wondered if the balloons had escaped from a child's hand, or slipped their knots from the front door of a house. They'd flown upwards and become tangled on a drainpipe. She focused on them until their edges blurred and they looked like poppies waving about in the breeze.

Her phone gave a low beep and it startled her. She grabbed it from her pocket. She expected it to be a message from her friend Tommy Eliot. She *hoped* it would be from him. The screen showed 'Mum' though. She was disappointed. Tommy had said he'd be around after school but hadn't shown. She'd waited in the common room for him for over half an hour. She opened the message.

Don't forget your doctor's appointment xxx

Mandy hadn't forgotten. She pushed her phone into her pocket impatiently and looked back to the house. In the corner of her eye the red balloons seemed to flicker.

Workmen had been in and out of the house for the last week or so. Mandy had found herself pausing at the site on her way to and from school. She'd stood watching as they came out carrying fireplaces and tiles and panes of leaded glass so that they could be resold. She saw bannisters and wooden doors put into the back of a lorry and then, bit by bit, the roof tiles came off, leaving the wooden beams exposed. The house had been stripped until it was just a shell.

It looked dead.

After the killing, five years ago, the property had been cordoned off with crime-scene tape and there had been police cars all along the street. Mandy had watched then too, standing on the opposite pavement with some other local kids. Her mother had become angry with her and insisted she come home. She'd said it was ghoulish, especially when the police began to dig up the back garden. But Mandy hadn't been able to stay away.

Now she was here again. Tommy had suggested she take a different route to school and back. She could have. She could have walked by the new estate and past the parade of shops that led to the Tube station. It would have taken a few minutes longer, but she could have cut this house out of her daily life.

She heard her ringtone, a soft warble coming from her pocket. She lifted it out and saw the name 'Tommy' on the screen. She smiled but didn't take the call. It was best not to be too available. Let Tommy think she had things to do, places to go, people to see.

She didn't want him to know where she really was.

She took a last look at the red balloons, straining in the breeze, and thought about Petra and Tina. Then she headed for the doctor's surgery.

Two

Dr Shukla had the results of Mandy's tests. She was staring at her computer screen and she tapped at her keyboard and made *um* noises at the same time. Her half-moon glasses had slipped down her nose.

'Bloods, normal.'

Mandy was sitting on the edge of her chair. The room was tiny, almost entirely taken up by the doctor's desk and an examination area. The only sound was the tapping of the keys.

'Now, what else? Urine, normal,' Dr Shukla said in a let's-get-down-to-business voice.

On the walls of the surgery were prints of famous paintings. Mandy's eye fixed on one she hadn't seen before. It was an image of a girl in a café late at night. Underneath were the words 'Edward Hopper, *Automat*'. The painting was new, she was sure. It was all dark shades, greens and browns. The girl was sitting at a table, alone. She had her hat and coat on and was drinking from a cup and saucer. The café seemed very peaceful. It was lit up but there were shadows across the floor. Outside the night was thick and black; only the lights of the café could be seen reflected on the glass.

'Chest X-ray, normal.'

The girl in the painting seemed totally alone in the world. Her face seemed intent on something. She was staring down at the cup, but Mandy imagined that her thoughts were far away. Mandy wondered why she was there. Her clothes were heavy, which suggested that it was winter. Her coat and hat were old fashioned and so was the decor of the café. What was the girl sitting there for? At that time of night? Mandy searched the picture for a suitcase but she couldn't see one.

She realised that Dr Shukla was staring at her.

'You are in good health, Mandy, although you look a little thin.'

'I don't have anorexia if that's what you think.'

The words had come out rudely, in a way she hadn't meant. She ate what she felt like eating. Years ago she had been a little podgy and her mother had frowned whenever she reached for a second piece of cake or a handful of biscuits. There was a time, after Petra and Tina had gone, when her mother thought she was overeating because of what had happened. In those days the house was full of calorie-counting books and healthy snacks. Then, a year or so ago, Mandy suddenly seemed to grow taller and lose the padding she'd had. Now her mother frowned if she left some pasta or didn't want any breakfast. Her mother seemed determined to be unhappy about her appetite and had taken to baking cakes and puddings.

'I wasn't suggesting that you were anorexic,' Dr Shukla smiled. 'Appetite is often a barometer of general health. Perhaps you could describe these symptoms you've been experiencing again.'

Dr Shukla's long hair was tied back and rested on one shoulder. It hung like a horse's tail. Mandy could see a few grey hairs at the parting.

'I get this kind of aching in my legs and sometimes a weak feeling as if my legs might not hold me up. And headaches.'

Dr Shukla wasn't writing any of this down. She had her elbows on the desk and was resting her chin on her hands. Behind her glasses her eyes were huge and dark, her eyebrows pencilled into a thin line.

'And sometimes I think I might be asthmatic because I can't quite catch my breath. When I'm going to sleep at night I seem to be breathing very shallowly and I worry that no oxygen is getting to my lungs.'

Dr Shukla took a deep breath.

'Mandy, my dear, I am not saying that you don't have anything wrong with you. I wouldn't say that at all. But many of these symptoms are linked with depression and anxiety.'

'It's not that,' Mandy said, feeling the frustration building in her voice, 'I am not depressed. I know I've had my problems in the past . . .'

Mandy dropped into silence. Dr Shukla started to tidy up her desk. She squared off a couple of small pads and a block of Post-its. She lined up two pens so that they were parallel. All the while she looked as if she was thinking, glancing at her computer screen from time to time, weighing up what to say.

Mandy knew this because she'd been in this seat a number of times before.

'Two twelve-year-old girls, friends of yours, disappeared,' Dr Shukla said gently. 'The likelihood is that they were both killed. This was a terrible thing to happen. The worst thing that can happen to any family, any community, any friend. You were not with them when it happened and it has had a lasting effect on you. I have evidence of this in my notes. You have come to me from time to time with all sorts of ailments and the truth is these have almost always been driven by your anxiety about what happened to your friends. Now I suspect that the same thing is happening now. Am I right in thinking that it's almost five years since the girls went missing?'

'At the end of October.'

'Anniversaries are always difficult. Autumn nights, the smell of fireworks, Halloween. These are all things that will remind you. And maybe even the newspapers will have things to say. Five years is a kind of milestone.'

Mandy thought of the house. She pictured it in the dark waiting to be flattened. The windows empty like eye sockets. Black shadows flitting from room to room. Tomorrow it would be just a piece of land waiting to be built on. She felt herself getting emotional. She stared down at her lap, willing herself not to cry.

'I have a suggestion,' Dr Shukla said in her let's-get-organised voice. 'We have a new member of staff arriving, a PhD student who is looking at issues of anxiety and depression as they affect young people. She is hoping to work with some of our patients and I think you would be an ideal person for her to spend time with.'

'Like counselling? I had counselling at school . . .'

'This would be different. You are older now. The problems of older adolescents are much more linked to adult depression and anxiety. At least that's how this new researcher sees it. I think you should meet her and see if she can help you. Meanwhile, I'll monitor your physical health and if any of your symptoms deteriorate then I'll send you to see a specialist.'

Mandy opened her mouth to disagree but then thought about it for a second. The researcher was *new*, not someone from around here.

'How does that sound?'

'OK.'

'So, I will tell her about you and she will contact you regarding a meeting.'

Dr Shukla began tapping at her keyboard and Mandy knew that the consultation was over. She mumbled something and got up and left. As she went she could hear Dr Shukla calling over the intercom for her next patient.

Mandy went to bed late, long after her mum and dad. Their bedroom door was shut just after ten and Mandy made herself a hot drink and took it up to her room while she looked on Facebook. There was a lot going on. Tommy was in the middle of a number of discussions and several girls that she knew were giving him flirty answers. She felt her face screw up and pondered whether to join in. She closed her laptop though and went and sat on the bed. There, by her pillow, was her bead box; she'd left it there that morning. She pulled out some elastic string and then sorted through the compartments for a variety of different coloured beads.

Her mum had been pleased with Dr Shukla's suggestion of counselling. Her mum was always happy if Mandy was being looked after or monitored by some doctor or other.

Mandy threaded the beads onto the elastic. This would be a simple bracelet. Just something colourful on her wrist. She could tie the ends; no need to fiddle with clasps, not this late at night.

She pictured Dr Shukla and remembered all the visits she had made to her over the years. At first, her mother always came with her. She sat in the patient chair while Mandy stood beside her, her mother filling up every inch of the consulting room. Her mother then explained at length what Mandy was thinking and feeling and after she'd got all her words out Dr Shukla would always turn to Mandy and see what she had to say. In those days it had been so difficult to add anything because her mother seemed to have said it all.

Then, a couple of years ago, after her mother had explained about the rashes on Mandy's inner arms and the backs of her legs, Dr Shukla had interrupted her and said, 'Do you mind if I have a word with Mandy on her own?'

Her mother had been affronted by this and had mumbled out a number of words and phrases but Dr Shukla had stood up suddenly, something she hardly ever did, and edged round her desk using a let's-get-this-job-done kind of voice. 'Now, Mrs Crystal, you have a fantastic relationship with Mandy and if I am to get to grips with what is wrong with her then maybe I have to develop a relationship with her too.' She'd opened the door and stood holding it and her mother seemed to have no choice but to get up and go out. Dr Shukla went out too, closing the door behind her. There were whispered voices, then the doctor came back in and started to ask Mandy questions for what seemed like a long time.

That was when Mandy had told her about seeing Petra Armstrong on the bus.

She'd been scared when saying it, because to her it was a sign of madness. It really happened, though. Not once but three times. The first time she'd been sitting on a bus going towards Stratford, gazing out of the window. She'd hardly noticed a girl of her own age walking up the centre aisle. Then when she sat down Mandy glanced at her profile and there, around the jaw, in the long hair, she saw something familiar, and the more she looked the more it seemed that this girl was Petra Armstrong, a year after she'd gone missing. Mandy stared at her in a helpless way and missed her stop, determined to see where she got off. She saw her walk away towards the shopping centre. That first time Petra would have been thirteen years old. Then a year later there she was again, on another bus. She saw what looked like a fourteen-year-old girl in skinny jeans wearing a brilliant red top, like Petra and Tina used to wear when they were singing in their girl group, The Red Roses. The face had sharpened, the body was different. Where Petra had more of a child-shaped figure, this girl, on the bus, had small breasts and a way of standing that seemed to hint at a much older girl. That time Mandy had got off at her own stop, leaving her there on the bus.

A year later she'd seen her once more, coming down the stairs of a Routemaster that was going along Oxford Street. A thin girl with long curly hair who had been holding onto the rail and swaying from side to side with the movement of the bus, smiling widely to someone further up whose legs Mandy could just see. She appeared to be about fifteen and her lips were painted into a pout. She got off at the next stop and skipped in front of the bus across the road towards Debenhams.

Mandy never told anyone about these sightings.

For a while, after each time, she began to look for Petra on every bus journey she took. There were teenage girls of all sizes and shapes and she would look from face to face to see that tiny spark of familiarity but she never saw it again.

That was what she had told Dr Shukla.

It had been a kind of confession.

Am I going mad? Am I seeing things?

In her heart she'd known that each time it had been a different girl, not the same girl growing up from year to year. But for a few moments, on the bus, she had been convinced that it had been Petra. Dr Shukla had just shaken her head, her forehead lined with concern. *The mind is a powerful tool. It can turn your longing into something that seems real. When you are depressed, fixated on something, it can show you what you want to see.*

But the oddest thing of all was why she had only ever seen Petra. Never Tina.

Mandy picked up the beaded bracelet that she'd made. She checked that it fitted her wrist and fastened the ends of it. She held it up so that it caught the light from her bedside lamp. Some of the stones were red and glinted like rubies. She was reminded of the two balloons that had been caught on the drainpipe of the house that afternoon.

After speaking to Dr Shukla about the sightings she never saw any again, as if their talk had broken some kind of spell she'd been under. There'd been no sixteen- or seventeen-year-old Petra holding onto a bus pole or sandwiched up against a window, staring at her mobile. There'd been no Petra pushing the bell for the next stop and leaping off the bus and running away.

Petra was gone now and Mandy never wanted to see her again.

Three

There was a crowd of people watching in Princess Street when the demolition began. Mandy was there but she avoided eye contact with anyone. The detached house stood out from all the others. It was a different style and older than the semis nearby. It was a big house and for a while, after the killing, it had been turned into flats. The line of bells was still there, on the wall adjacent to the entrance. In the last couple of years it had been empty though, slowly falling apart, its brickwork fading, its front garden growing steadily, the plants and weeds creeping ever closer towards the house.

Now it was full of workmen and machinery.

A loud noise came from a yellow digger. It had caterpillar wheels like a tank and it moved delicately, turning a half circle in the confined space of the front garden. Metal jaws began to rise up as the arm of the vehicle swung into place. Mandy's eyes focused on the claw of the machine as it bit into the top of the brick wall with a crunching noise. There was a silence for a second. She held her breath as the masonry fell away, pulling part of the top bay window with it. It crashed to the ground causing a flurry of dust.

Mandy pulled the edges of her hood forward, hoping that no one would notice her, but everybody was looking towards the house, concentrating on the activity there.

Mandy toyed with the bracelet she had on. She rotated it gently round her wrist, feeling the different shapes and textures of the beads she'd strung there the night before.

'Hello, Mandy,' came a voice from behind her.

Mandy tensed, reluctant to get into a conversation with anyone. The people who lived round here knew who she was and knew about her link to the house. The last thing she wanted was any sympathetic comments. She turned slightly and saw a man in a suit. He had grey, almost white, hair. He was holding car keys and the rain that had just started was dotting his jacket. It didn't look as though he'd prepared himself for the weather.

'Officer Farraday,' she said.

She hadn't seen him for a number of years but still she knew him straight away. She heard the other officers call him Colin but she had always called him Officer.

'Not on duty,' he said. 'Just Colin today.'

'Not on official business then?'

Why did she say that? *Official business?* Tommy would have rolled his eyes.

Officer Farraday shook his head, glancing from time to time at the house.

'What are you doing these days? You must be . . . what? In the sixth form now?'

'I am. Taking A levels.'

'But not in school today.'

'No, I'm going in later. Why have you come?'

It was a silly question. He was there for the same reason she was.

'I passed by a couple of days ago and saw that the house was fenced off. I enquired and found out that it was being demolished today. I spent enough time in that house. I felt I should see it go down.'

Mandy understood. The two of them had connections to this old building. There was a difference though. Officer Farraday had spent a lot of time *in* the house whereas she had never set foot inside. Not once.

'I expect you have strong feelings about the place as well,' Officer Farraday said.

She nodded.

'Do you still think about them, Mandy?' Officer Farraday said.

'Sometimes.'

Mandy thought about them *a lot*.

'The case is still open. There's nothing worse than an unsolved case. Especially when it concerns the probable death of two little girls.'

'They won't find anything now, though, will they? Not after all this time.' Mandy looked at the officer.

'There are reports of sightings of the two girls. Even now.'

'But they never come to anything?' she said, thinking, for a moment, about her own *sightings*.

'No. But never say never. Their bodies weren't found. The two girls could still be alive. There have been cases in the USA where girls were abducted and kept captive for many years and then found a way to escape.'

That was true. Mandy had read of such a case recently. A man held three young girls captive in his house in Cleveland, Ohio. She had watched the reports on the news for days. He kept them for ten years. He imprisoned them in a cellar and one of them had a baby. One day, while he was out, one of the girls broke out through the front door and ran to a neighbour's house crying and begging for help. She made a phone call to the police and they played it on the news. Mandy had listened in amazement at the girl's frantic attempt to alert the police before her kidnapper returned. Her voice was thin and stretched, like it might break at any point. 'I've been kidnapped and I've been missing for ten years. And I'm . . . I'm here. I'm free now.' Mandy had gone onto the internet and listened to the recording over and over. She'd tried to picture the girl clutching onto the neighbour's phone, her eyes darting here and there, still afraid that her freedom might be snatched away at any moment.

She'd thought of Petra and Tina. Who wouldn't have?

Officer Farraday crossed his arms. Without his uniform he looked like someone who might work in a building society. She wondered why he was wearing a suit on his day off.

'Without a body you can never be sure that someone is really dead.' He said it thoughtfully. Maybe he too was thinking of the Cleveland case.

The rain had lessened and the digger was continuing its work. It had moved to the side and its jaws were pulling at the guttering. Mandy remembered the two red balloons that had been trapped there the day before. There was no sign of them now. A corner of the wall suddenly came away and fell.

18

The roof beams were leaning to one side as the digger went in again, the metal pushing against the wall. Moments later it collapsed, sending out a shower of small stones and dust.

'I half expected to see Alison Pointer here,' Officer Farraday said. 'But I suppose she's too busy with her group and her talks. I saw her on television a couple of weeks ago. Did you?'

'No,' Mandy said.

Mandy knew that Alison Pointer, Tina's mum, had been on television. It was a programme that was looking at the girls' disappearance. *Five Years On* it was called. She'd chosen not to watch it.

'Well, look at that. I did *not* expect to see him,' Officer Farraday said.

Mandy turned in the direction of his gaze. Further along the street, standing back from other people, was Jason Armstrong, Petra's father. Mandy looked him over. He was thin-faced and looked ill. His hair was long and straggly and he was wearing a huge overcoat, which hung off his shoulders. He had one elbow leaning on the roof of a car. He wasn't looking at anyone, just staring at the old house.

'Where does he live now?'

'Not sure. I do know he's done a few stints in prison. Twelve months for aggravated burglary and a couple of short stays for other things. He's a drunk. Always was. I don't know why social workers ever let Petra live with him.'

Now Jason Armstrong was looking in their direction. He seemed puzzled. Mandy wondered if he recognised her. She'd changed in five years but maybe not that much. She caught his eye for a few moments then looked away.

'I must go,' Officer Farraday said. 'I'm glad to hear you're doing well.'

She watched him walk away. There was a kind of spring in his step as he headed for a car further up the street. Maybe coming here had made him feel better, as if he'd paid his respects.

She looked back to the demolition. Most of the roof had come down. A bulldozer was pushing a heap of rubble away from the house to give the digger room to move further around. A downstairs window frame was half hanging out, the net curtain still strung across the middle.

Mandy decided to go. She'd get to school for her second class. She had plenty of time but had had enough of standing in the street dredging up the past. She remembered something Dr Shukla had said over and over. *It's time to move on. The past is done, finished.*

She saw that Petra's father was also walking away. It would be easy for her to catch up with him, say something sympathetic. Her conversation with Officer Farraday hadn't troubled her at all. But Petra's dad was something else. He had always been a distant man. The few times she'd seen him in his cab or talking to Petra, he'd all but ignored her. Not like Alison Pointer, who made the most enormous fuss over Tina's friends.

Jason Armstrong turned just then and saw her. He stopped and leant against the wall. He was clearly waiting for her. She couldn't change direction because it would be obvious that she was avoiding him. She walked on, steeling herself.

'Hello, Mr Armstrong. How are you?' she said.

'Not so good,' he said.

'I'm sorry to hear that.'

'You're Mandy, aren't you? All grown up now. A young woman.'

She smiled awkwardly, not knowing how to answer him.

'I expect you feel relieved when you look at that house,' he said.

He pulled a handkerchief from the pocket of his overcoat. It was cotton, and bunched up as if it had been used many times. He blew his nose on it. Mandy felt marooned. She couldn't walk on because they were in the middle of a conversation of some sort and it would be rude. She placed her hand on her bracelet, rubbing a couple of the beads with her fingers.

'You didn't go in there, did you? That was sensible.'

'I have to go. I've got to get to school.'

His eyes looked empty and he smelt faintly of alcohol. The way he said 'sensible' implied some criticism. As if she should have gone in there after them.

He wasn't to know how often she wished that she had.

She walked off, leaving the noise of the demolition behind her.

Four

Mandy went into school using the visitor's entrance. She passed by a small car park where the Head's car and those of the senior teachers were parked. She walked towards the reception doors and was about to press the keypad when she paused and looked round at the small garden area that was set apart on the other side. It had once been part of the car park but was now a half circle of grass backed by a brick wall. The Head called it a 'remembrance garden'.

Mandy walked across to it. The grass area was small but there were four pots with miniature bushes planted in them. They looked formal and upright, the foliage trimmed so that each one was exactly the same height and shape. In the summer the garden looked more vibrant with flowers and hanging baskets that hooked onto the wall. Then it was bright and pretty. Now it seemed bare and there were drifts of brown leaves between the grass and the wall that had blown there from nearby trees. The wall itself was curved along the top. In the middle of it was a copper plaque for Petra and Tina. Mandy looked at it. It was solid, square. The words on it were simple.

The plaque had flowers engraved around the edge, rosebuds; blooms that had not yet reached their prime.

The garden and the plaque had been unveiled exactly one year after they had gone missing. There'd been a ceremony where all the students from the school had filed into the small car park and stood in silence while prayers were said. Tina's parents had been there but Jason Armstrong was absent. Poems had been read out and Alison Pointer had made a short speech about the importance of memory and how people were never really gone if they were still in the minds of their friends and families. She also said that she would never stop looking for the two girls.

Mandy had been at the edge of the front row and had stifled a sob at that point. The rest of the class looked serious and solemn but she wondered if any of them really cared. It had been a year since it happened and the girls had disappeared only eight weeks after school had started. There had hardly been time for the form class to bond, to become friends. There had been tears, Mandy had seen them, but they quickly dried up as friends comforted each other and enjoyed a few minutes of drama at the expense of two girls whom they'd hardly known and perhaps hadn't even liked very much.

Mandy had liked them. Mandy had wanted to be their friend and be part of their girl group, The Red Roses.

The sound of some students coming through the car park broke her reverie. She looked round and they gave her a wave. Jon Wallis was with them. He was in the upper sixth and lived in her street. He'd been really friendly and helpful to her during the summer holidays when he found out she was staying on in the sixth form. For a while she had thought they might get together but that was before Tommy Eliot turned up. She gave Jon a smile and waved at the others. They didn't stop to speak to her, probably aware that she was looking at the garden, thinking that maybe she was praying for her lost friends.

A lot of students in her year were like that. Even now, five years later, they tiptoed round the subject in case they might offend or upset her. It was one of the reasons she liked Tommy so much. He'd gone to a different senior school but joined their sixth form at the beginning of term. He didn't have the shared history that she had with the other students. He was an outsider and that was why she felt relaxed talking to him.

He was the one person she could talk to about Petra and Tina.

She went on to the sixth form common room. Her class wasn't until eleven fifteen. There were a few students dotted about and she could hear snatches of music escaping from various sets of headphones. She got herself a drink from the dispenser and sat down. She blew across the top of the cup and saw that there were ten minutes or so to go before the current lesson ended. It was history and she usually sat with Tommy at the side of the classroom next to the window. If she was late he would save a seat for her and vice versa. Today he wouldn't have bothered because she'd texted him to say she was going to the house, to watch the start of the demolition.

He would miss her, she thought. He was always writing notes on bits of paper and passing them to her. He liked to comment on the clothes the teacher was wearing or the mood they were in. Then he wrote completely irrelevant points about things that were going on in the world. Once or twice he put little kisses at the bottom of the note and she felt embarrassed by them and found herself looking out of the window in case she blushed and he noticed.

She remembered the first time she ever saw him. It was at the preliminary meeting of the new sixth form intake where Miss Pearce was welcoming them all. He came in a few minutes late. Mandy was on the end of a row but there was a spare seat next to her so she moved along and let him sit down.

She was startled by his appearance.

He had longish hair and wore a suit jacket over skinny trousers and patterned DMs. The buttons of the jacket were done up to the top. Underneath there was a glimpse of a silver T-shirt. On the floor was a briefcase. It was made from hard brown leather and seemed sturdy and old fashioned, something a boy from a private school might carry.

He looked so different to the other boys in the sixth form. Finally after five years of blazers and dark trousers they were allowed to wear their own clothes. Most of them had on jeans and sports tops and trainers. They'd gone from one uniform to another. Mandy was no different. She wore jeans and a T-shirt, not unlike the other girls in the sixth form.

Tommy was completely unselfconscious about how he looked and had taken a large pad out of his briefcase and was making notes about what Miss Pearce was saying. He was the only one taking notes. After the talk Mandy noticed some of the boys looking at him warily or dismissively. Tommy seemed unconcerned and struck up conversations with anyone who wanted to talk to him.

He talked to Mandy for ages and he told her how he was looking forward to university so that he could live away from home and make all his own decisions. He was going to be a journalist, he said, and expose wrongdoing. He'd seemed a little intense then, but he cheered up quickly and made jokes about his old school. The next day, at the first lesson of her English course, he was there early and called to her, 'I've saved you a seat!' And she sat beside him and they became friends.

They'd been like that for seven weeks and during that time her feelings had grown and become something else. Every day she looked forward to seeing him and felt aggrieved if he wasn't around. When she was with him the day seemed brighter somehow, with stacks of time for doing things. She even *looked* better, her hair fuller, her smile wider. She longed to tell him, to say something to him about the way he made her feel but she did not know where to start. On good days she thought that the same thing might be happening to him. He was instantly popular and chatted to loads of people but he always seemed to look for her as if she were his anchor. If she was around he seemed to feel a need to touch her: lightly on the shoulder, his fingers on her arm, a loose clasp of her wrist or a pat on her back.

He was genuinely interested in her. He knew about the missing girls, he'd passed the remembrance garden often enough, but when he realised she had been the third girl he was shocked and full of sympathy. To other kids the story was old news but to him it was as if it had happened the previous week.

The buzzer went for the change of lessons, followed by the noise of doors opening and voices spilling out into the corridors. In moments the sound was louder, as if someone had turned the volume up. The common-room door burst open and several students came in, some chattering, some shrieking, others looking at their mobiles.

Tommy appeared. He looked round the common room and smiled when he saw her.

'Hi,' he said. 'You didn't miss much in history . . .'

She smiled.

'See the house demolished?'

'Yeah.'

He sat down in the next seat, his legs straight out in front of him. He was humming under his breath. He'd moved on from the comment he'd just made. It was another reason why she liked him. He didn't dwell on her bad experiences. He was upbeat, ready to change the subject. She appreciated that. With him she felt there was the possibility that she could enjoy herself again.

He was wearing a Fair Isle jumper and loose jeans with plimsolls. His briefcase was sitting on the floor between them. He didn't look like anyone else in the sixth form. She knew his clothes were from charity shops. He created his own style and boasted that he almost never wore anything that was new. She looked down at her own clothes: dark trousers and the hoodie she had worn to the demolition. Underneath it was a black T-shirt. Not exactly imaginative. *She* had no style at all but his clothes seemed to tell some kind of story. She wasn't quite sure yet what that story was.

'History was full of the usual stuff. Imperialism and the Scramble for Africa. Got a couple of new essay titles. I've made notes.'

'On a memory stick?'

'No. With a pen. On a piece of paper. I told you I remember it better if I actually write it down. I can photocopy it for you?'

'I can't read your writing.'

'I'll go through it with you.'

'A memory stick would be easier.'

'It's a bit of a misnomer, really. A memory stick that *remembers* nothing. It should be called a copy stick, as in, there's a *copy* of what you want on this.'

Mandy sighed. It was so easy to get into some kind of profound conversation with Tommy. On the other hand it was difficult not to admire his passion for stuff, even something simple like a conversation about history notes. He was always involved in something. One week he was making music videos, the next he was setting up a joint blog and taking part in writing a novel set in the distant future.

'You do the Shakespeare essay?' he said, gulping down some water from a bottle.

'I made a start.'

'It's due in tomorrow.'

'I know. I'll get an extension.'

'Isn't that just piling it up to be done later? *To-morrow, and to-morrow, and to-morrow.*'

'You sound like Miss Pearce.'

'That reminds me, there was something I wanted to ask you.'

He picked up his briefcase and sorted through some papers. It was always full of handouts and pages of notes. He religiously printed everything out. 'I don't trust computers!' he'd said over and over. Now he pulled some sheets of paper from a folder and handed them to her. Mandy was expecting some notes from the session she'd missed. Instead it was a printout of a newspaper report. 'Mystery of Missing Girls' was the heading.

'What's this?' she said, even though she knew full well what it was.

'Miss Pearce has asked me to do a talk about it. For the fifth anniversary.'

The fifth anniversary was in two weeks.

'It's just for the sixth form. I think I've been asked to do it because I'm one of the few people who weren't in the school at the time it happened. Thing is I feel a bit awkward about it. I wasn't sure whether you'd be all right with me doing it.'

'Why wouldn't I be?'

Miss Pearce had talked to her about it a couple of weeks before. She'd said she planned to ask Tommy to do it and hoped that Mandy wouldn't mind.

'I just wanted to check with you. And, she also wants me to write something for the school website. I've been doing some research, I mean, I know you told me all about it but I thought I'd better read up on stuff. Those are some of the documents that I've downloaded. If you're all right with what's there then I can use them for my research. I hoped you wouldn't mind looking through and just telling me if they're accurate.'

29

She frowned at the papers in her hand. He looked worried.

'You want me to tell Miss Pearce I won't do it? I don't want to upset you,' he said, reaching across and touching her hand.

'Don't be silly. I've got a free period after English. I'll look these over and give them back to you at lunch.'

'Thanks.'

The common room door opened and Toni and Leanne came in. They walked straight over to Tommy and Mandy and began talking breathlessly about a party that was happening on Saturday.

'Zoe, in business studies? Her mum and dad are away at the weekend but her older brother is there and he says he'll make sure the party doesn't get out of hand. We've been invited and you guys as well,' Toni said, looking from Tommy to Mandy and back again.

Tommy immediately started to talk about the party. Toni and Leanne pulled up chairs. Mandy folded the papers he'd given her and slid them into her bag. She slipped away while they were all talking.

'Wait,' he called.

She turned round and saw him walk towards her. Leanne and Toni looked a bit miffed.

'The thing is . . . I might not have explained it all that well but this talk I'm going to give is meant to be a sort of final goodbye to the girls? And that will mean that you can surely put it all in the past? What with the demolition and this. It'll all be gone for you. You can get on with your life.'

He was looking right into her eyes. She softened. He had it all worked out.

'Course,' she said. 'I'll look at the stuff and get back to you.'

'You will come to this party on Saturday? It'll be fun.'

'Probably,' she said.

Walking away, along the corridor, she thought about what he'd said about her getting on with her life. *You can surely put it in the past*. 'The past'; as if it were a box of some sort in which she could lock away troublesome things. He wasn't to know how often people had said this to her. It wasn't his fault that he was just echoing words that she'd heard for years.

Everyone wanted her to move on. Maybe one day she would.

Five

•

After art, Mandy found a quiet carrel in the library and sat down. There were other students about, some with headphones on, most of them focused on writing or reading. She pulled out the printouts that Tommy had given her. She flicked through. They were in date order: the top one was the oldest, from a few days after Petra and Tina had gone missing. 'Mystery of Missing Girls Deepens.'

The text was simple and straightforward and summed up the facts of the story.

At five o'clock on Thursday 28th October, 2010, two twelve-year-old friends, Petra Armstrong and Tina Pointer, entered a house in Princess Street, Holloway, North London. A third girl, unnamed, was due to accompany them but did not.

The house was owned by George Merchant, seventy-nine, a retired accountant. Sources say that Merchant's health had been poor and he was mostly housebound. He lived in one room of the large property and the girls, according to their friend, were intent on exploring the dilapidated building. There had been talk of ghosts and hauntings.

When police entered the property they found George Merchant dead from head injuries. The place had been ransacked and there was evidence of theft. There was no sign of the girls. Forensic examination of the house is continuing. An extensive search of the property and the garden is still ongoing. As yet there is no information on the fate of Petra and Tina. A nationwide search has been set up and their pictures circulated in the media and on social networking sites.

In the middle of the article were school photographs of Petra and Tina: small rectangular pictures of two smiling girls, taken a few weeks before they went missing. The photographer had come into school in the early weeks of term. Mandy looked at Petra's photograph. Her hair was long and parted in the middle. It hung smoothly down each side of her face. She had a half smile. She looked demure, shy even. How different to the photos of her dressed up in her girl-band outfit. The Red Roses pictures were posed and showed a made-up face with white teeth. Then Petra looked pouty and grown-up. In real life Petra didn't smile a lot. She seemed to spend a lot of time chewing at the side of her lip.

Mandy focused on the picture of Tina. Tina always looked the same. She had curly hair which she held back in hairslides or hairbands. Her smile was wide, showing dimples on each cheek. Her eyes were bright, as if someone were holding a gift for her that she was just about to open. Her Red Roses pictures were exactly the same. Tina was Tina but Petra had different faces that she showed to different people.

Mandy carried on reading the article.

The two girls have vanished. The police are following various lines of enquiry. Although these two girls are very young, there is the possibility that they have run away and are hiding. Police forces all over the south-east are asking holiday-home owners to search their properties and outbuildings. The police say they are robustly pursuing their investigations.

Mandy remembered this story. In the days after the girls went missing there were constant reminders for people to check their outbuildings, sheds, empty flats, holiday homes. Mandy had been baffled by this. She had seen the two girls go into the house. She had told the police this. Why would the police think that they had come out of it again and run away? Mandy remembered Tina had been wearing an old hoodie, the sleeves too long; it looked as though it belonged to her mother. Petra had on a light jacket and was shivering as she stood on the street.

Why would Petra and Tina have gone into the house, come back out again and then, on a moment's whim, decided to run away to the country? How could they have been hiding, unnoticed, in some flat or cottage or caravan? Something inside her had told her firmly that this wasn't what had happened. Five years later it sounded just as preposterous.

The next article Tommy had printed off was from a few days later. This was when the police had a new theory. Mandy remembered the excitement of her mother and father when this news had spread. It seemed like a possible answer.

Missing Girls May Have Witnessed Murder

Despite a nationwide search, there are still no clues to the whereabouts of Petra Armstrong and Tina Pointer. The two twelve year olds went into the house of an elderly man on October 28th and have not been seen since.

At a press conference late last night Chief Inspector Malcolm Roberts made a statement. 'It is our conviction that the events that took place in 58 Princess Street may have happened simultaneously. That is to say the murder of Mr George Merchant may have taken place in the same window of time that the two young girls entered the house. In this case we are looking into the theory that the two girls could have witnessed the murder of Mr George Merchant by a person or persons unknown. This may have provoked an abduction of the girls and for this reason we believe that the girls may be being held against their will in some unspecified location.'

Appeals to the public have identified a van that was parked outside the property on the night of the incident.

Police say that investigations into Mr Merchant's past show that, as an accountant, he had dealings with some clients who were linked to organised crime. 'This could have been a payback killing for some wrongdoing,' Chief Inspector Roberts said.

Meanwhile police are looking for a white Ford van with a scrape along the driver's side and possibly a 2007 registration plate. They are also asking the public to be vigilant and report any unusual activity in their local vicinity.

Mandy sat back. She pulled at the chain around her neck. There was a piece of amber on it that her mother had given her from an old brooch that she'd found in a collectibles market. Mandy had made it into a pendant. It felt slippery under her fingers and she pulled it up and pressed it to her lips.

The police's theory had had a real ring of the truth about it. Mandy had thought about it for hours, days, weeks afterwards. She had left Petra and Tina on the street minutes before they crept into the side gate of the house. What if they had stumbled upon someone killing Mr Merchant? Might that person (or more than one person) have panicked and taken them away somewhere? Could they be holding them until they decided what to do with them?

In the next few days there was speculation on the television news. There were press appeals. The police made several re-enactments of what they thought had happened. They had three twelve-year-old girls walk along Princess Street and then one of them walk off while the other two headed towards the house. It was dark though, and most people were at home and not in the street, so Mandy couldn't see how anyone would remember anything. The police were adamant that it had 'yielded fresh clues and new information'.

Now Mandy looked at the article again. She flicked through a couple of the others behind it. She began to feel a bit irked. It was on her mind too much. Why had Tommy downloaded all this stuff? How was it relevant to a talk at a memorial service? The facts were simple. Two girls had disappeared. There was no explanation. What else did Tommy need to know in order to give a talk to the sixth form? Then she remembered he was also writing something on it for the school website. She sighed.

When she left Tommy in the common room he was being monopolised by Toni and Leanne. She wondered if he had sat near them in sociology. She pictured them perching either side of him protectively. She wished, not for the first time, that she had chosen sociology as one of her subjects.

She turned crossly to the back pages. Tommy had included a longer, more serious piece, perhaps from a Sunday supplement. The date at the top was June 2011, eight months afterwards. Most of the newspapers had stopped reporting the story by then, though there was one that had lurid headlines every couple of weeks or so. She remembered some of the headlines: 'Moth Girls Abducted from House'; 'Girls Drawn to the House'; 'Moth Girls Besotted by Gloomy House'; 'Mystery House Holds Its Grisly Secrets'.

The Moth Girls.

She hadn't thought of that phrase for years.

It gave her an unpleasant feeling. She hadn't liked it at the time. She didn't like moths. They made her shiver. They came into her room on a summer night and were sucked towards the light, sometimes throwing themselves against lampshades, making scuttling noises with their wings. They were dark and hairy-looking, and sat on walls in high-up places where they couldn't be shooed away. They only seemed to come out when it was dark, stealthy and foreboding.

The press called Petra and Tina 'Moth Girls' because they had been attracted to the house. They were drawn to it. Though Mandy hated the phrase she couldn't dispute the truth of it. Right from the moment that she'd started to hang out with the girls, Petra had talked and talked about going into the house in Princess Street. Tina never said much about it but she usually did whatever Petra wanted her to do.

Her eye skimmed over the Sunday supplement article but she didn't take any of it in. She was upset. She was also a little bit angry. Why was she even reading this stuff? She packed it all away in her bag and got up and walked out of the library.

She headed for the lunch rooms and when she got there she looked around for Tommy. He was in the far corner at a table with Toni and Leanne. Zoe was there as well with some boys Mandy didn't know. She saw, from across the room, that Tommy was sitting smack in the middle of the group and he was talking about something. The other students were staring at him, hanging on his every word. The sight of it gave her a twinge in her chest. Tommy was popular. He was easy to get on with. That's why everyone else liked him. People like Tommy had to be shared around.

He noticed her standing there and got up and walked towards her. The others looked round. Their faces did not have the same welcoming look. Mandy stood where she was. She had no intention of encroaching on their gathering.

'Hi,' she said, pulling the papers out of her bag. 'I've looked at these. They all seem pretty accurate.'

She handed them to him.

'I'll show you my speech when I've written it.'

'No need.'

He was bristling, like a puppy. He was pleased with his task and wanted to do it well.

'Zoe was just telling us about the party. You're coming, right?'

'I don't know, maybe.'

He stepped closer to her and put his hand on her elbow.

'It wouldn't be the same if you weren't there.'

She felt her knees soften. His fingers on her arm were warm and she longed to place her hand on top of them.

'I'll probably be able to come,' she said.

'Great. Thanks for looking at these,' he said and walked away.

Six

Late Friday afternoon, when Mandy got in, she could hear Alison Pointer's voice from the kitchen. She was talking to her mother. Dismayed, Mandy stood in the hallway and listened for a moment to see how the conversation sounded. She had bought some new clothes for Zoe's party the following evening. Buying them had made her feel good, but now Alison was here she found herself looking at them with a feeling of guilt. Alison's visits were never predictable. On some days she was upset, crying, pulling tissues from a box one after the other. Other times she was fine, brisk and business-like, outlining plans for some project she was involved in.

Mandy listened hard. Today Alison sounded upbeat. She relaxed.

'Mandy, is that you?' her mother called out.

'It is. I'll be there in a minute.'

She went upstairs and threw her bags into her room. Then she came back down to the kitchen. Alison was sitting at the kitchen table, looking smart in dark trousers and a cream jumper. On the floor, by her chair, was a large leather handbag. It sat up on the ground like a stiff case. A leather coat hung untidily over the back of an adjacent chair. Mandy could see that Alison's nails had been painted dark red. She looked like she'd just come from a television interview. When Mandy first knew her she dressed like her own mum except on the days when she was a receptionist in the doctor's. Now she was usually beautifully turned out.

Her mother was in jeans and a loose shirt. There were mixing bowls on the side and packets of flour. She was baking again. No doubt there would be a Victoria sponge or a Madeira cake for her to nibble at later.

'Mandy! How are you?' Alison said, smiling widely.

'Hello, Alison,' she said.

It had taken Mandy a long time to be able to call Mrs Pointer 'Alison'. She pulled out a kitchen chair and sat down.

'Did you see the demolition? My neighbour tells me it's all flat now.'

'I was there for a while on Tuesday morning but I've not been past it since. I've been going to school a different way so I haven't seen –'

'I deliberately didn't go,' Alison said. 'I couldn't face it. I've walked past that house many times over the years and sometimes I found it a bit of a comfort, knowing that it was the last place Tina had been. I was afraid, you know, that I might try to stop them knocking it down. Which is ridiculous. If ever there's a house I should loathe and hate it's that one.'

'I saw Jason Armstrong there just as they were starting on the demolition,' Mandy said.

Alison's face darkened. 'What did he have to say?'

'I spoke to him briefly,' Mandy said, remembering his words and how they had upset her. 'He looked rough.'

41

'Living in a hostel, I heard, in East London somewhere. A complete loser.'

'Maybe losing Petra . . .'

'He was always a complete loser. Do you know, after the girls went missing I asked him to get involved with the campaign to help find them and he refused. Just point-blank said, "No thanks!" Can you believe that? In the last five years he never lifted a finger to help with the publicity or raising awareness. Oh, don't get me started on Jason Armstrong!'

'They did say that the family were "known to the social services",' her mum said.

'I always knew that. We had their notes in the surgery. I didn't look until after it happened but I knew he had his problems. Why do you think I never let my Tina stay round there? Why do you think all the sleepovers were at my place?'

'And here,' her mum said. 'The girls stayed here once.'

'Course! I was quite happy for Tina to stay here. I knew she was safe here.'

'Alison's had some amazing news,' her mother said.

'Oh?'

Alison always had lots of things to talk about. She was on committees that dealt with child protection and child safety issues. She'd also created a national website called Safe and Sound, which was a way of swapping information about missing children.

'There have been some sightings of someone who looks a lot like Tina,' Alison said quietly.

'Sightings? Again?'

'I know there's been a number over the years but these have a real feeling of authenticity. In the last week I've been

42

contacted by three people in an area of thirteen square kilometres, in France, outside a town called Bergerac. It's very rural there. Here is the really exciting thing. One of them sent a photograph.'

'A picture?'

Alison's eyes were shining.

'I'll show you,' she said and rummaged about in her bag. She pulled out an iPad and tapped the screen several times. 'Here.'

Mandy took the iPad. Onscreen she saw a blurred picture of a teenage girl standing by a car on a garage forecourt. She was leaning on the roof of the car and staring into the distance. Beside it, slightly smaller, was a head-and-shoulder shot of a teenage girl. She had curly hair held back with pins and dimples in her cheeks. There was a similarity about the two girls.

'The other picture is the computer-enhanced image of Tina. We have that done every six months. It's a version of what she might look like now. Of course, we have one of Petra too. Actually we have updated pictures of over twenty children on the website. Hard to believe that there are so many missing. So many unhappy families.'

Mandy looked at her mother. She appeared uncomfortable, using her nail to scratch at something on the surface of the table. These conversations with Alison always led to heavy silences. Alison's broken heart was there in the room with them; no one could say anything to make it any better.

'But *these* sightings have been of Tina,' Alison said. 'So I'm very excited. Three sightings in one week. The police are extremely interested and the French police are being helpful. I'm flying out there tomorrow.'

Mandy nodded her head positively. She had an image in her head of Alison sitting in an aisle seat, coupling the seat belt neatly across her middle and saying to the person next to her, 'I'm going to find my daughter.'

'It could be good news,' Mandy said.

'Yes,' Alison said.

She picked up her iPad and stared at the picture. She raised her finger as if to slide it across the screen or tap to change the app. Instead she let it hover over the image of the girl on the garage forecourt, her ruby-coloured fingernail drooping as if it could actually touch the face.

'This could be a breakthrough,' she said, almost under her breath. 'This could be something important. Not just for Tina but for Petra too.'

'The police will follow it up,' her mother said. 'There's loads of cooperation between police forces of different countries now.'

There had been a number of days like this when Alison had come into their house and shared news with them of a false dawn. The early sightings were many. The girls had been seen in Leicester, Durham, Glasgow. They'd been seen abroad: Portugal, France, Majorca, the Canary Islands. All those places that were brimming with English tourists who looked around and fixed their gaze on any pair of girls who might fit the description. They didn't deliberately mislead; they wanted, more than anything, to be right. They wanted to find these two sweet girls and return them to their families. Lead after lead was followed up and each proved to be false. As the years passed by the leads diminished, the case wound down, the mystery deepened. What had become of them?

Mandy thought of the girls locked in the cellar in Cleveland, Ohio. She wondered what had gone through Alison's mind when she'd read about that case.

'I should go,' Alison said. 'Loads to do. I'll let you both know about the France thing. Although,' she said, her voice a little lower, 'if it *is* Tina, well . . . I don't know how I'll be. On the other hand, if it's not . . . I might be in a worse state.'

'I'll see you out,' Mandy said.

Alison pushed her iPad into her bag and straightened her trouser creases. She picked up her coat from the back of the chair.

'Keep your fingers crossed for me!'

'We always do,' her mother said.

Mandy walked out into the hall and opened the front door. The cold air slipped into the house.

Alison paused for a second to put her coat on. She did all the buttons up and tied the belt. Then she turned to the hall mirror and had a look at herself. When she'd finished she took a step towards the front door. She hesitated though, making an 'Oh!' sound as if she'd forgotten something. Mandy expected her to go back into the kitchen to pick up some item from the table or share some last-minute piece of gossip with her mother. Instead she stepped close to Mandy and clasped her arm with her hand. She spoke quietly in her ear as if she didn't want her mother to hear.

'And you know, Mandy, I don't blame you any more,' she said, squeezing her arm. 'I may have said a few things all those years ago. I may have been unkind to you then. Said things I shouldn't have said. You were a child though. It wasn't your fault. I don't hold you responsible any more. Not one bit.'

Mandy didn't answer. She gave a weak smile and Alison went out of the house with a backwards wave. When Mandy shut the door she felt something heavy clamp across her shoulders. Her mother was always saying that. 'It's not your fault, Mandy.'

But Mandy blamed herself. She always had and she always would.

Seven

Later that evening, when her parents were watching television, Mandy went into her room and shut the door. Alison's comments to her had been playing round her head all night. She hadn't eaten much and had had to fend off questions about her lack of appetite from her mother. She helped with the dishes and then had a bath. In her room, she answered some texts on her phone, three from Tommy and a couple from some other girls. She put her new clothes onto a hanger – a red top and black jeans – and hooked it onto the outside of her wardrobe door so that she could look at it. She placed the shoes underneath. They were red like the top and had high heels. She turned them over, wondering if she'd made a good choice. After a while she tidied up her bead box, sorting out clasps and wires so that she could make a necklace. She was all fingers and thumbs though and it was hard to thread the beads so she shoved them back into the box and shut the lid with a bang. Then she tried to think about Zoe's party the following evening. Tommy's texts had been about making arrangements to go.

What time are you thinking of getting there?

Are you bringing booze?

Should we meet up?

But she couldn't stop thinking about what Alison had said.

In the end she lay back on her bed and thought about her short friendship with Petra and Tina. It had lasted barely seven weeks and yet it seemed the defining thing about her teenage years.

She remembered the first day in secondary school and how she had ended up sitting alongside them. The class was full of small knots of children who were sticking by the kids they'd known in primary school. She was the odd one out. Miss Pearce made Petra and Tina move their bags off the adjacent seat so that Mandy could sit down. Tina was nice. Mandy's family had moved into a house further down Tina's street in the summer and her mum had become quite friendly with Tina's mum. Petra was reserved though. She did a lot of shoulder shrugging and looking away across the room as if Mandy weren't there.

At home time Mandy walked along with them. They stayed together for a while until Petra had to go off down her street. Then Tina was more lively and chatty and told Mandy stuff about her dad who lived in South London with a beautician. When they got to Tina's house she said, 'See you tomorrow,' in a friendly way.

The next day though Mandy got the cold shoulder from Petra and awkward half smiles from Tina. Even though she sat at their table and walked around with them to other classes she felt like she was hanging on. It wasn't until lunchtime that they began to warm up. They were going to have a rehearsal for their girl group, The Red Roses, and asked Mandy if she would look after their stuff. Then she was allowed to sit in the gym and listen as they sang their songs, three of them. Petra was showing Tina some new dance moves and Mandy gave a clap after they finished their songs.

That night, on the way home, Petra said, loudly and clearly, 'You can't be in our band. It's a duo. Just the two of us!' But Mandy knew already that she couldn't be in their band. Petra and Tina were skinny and could wear tight-fitting clothes, but Mandy was chunky and liked to wear heavy jumpers over loose jeans.

It was an unequal friendship, as if Petra and Tina were in a boat and Mandy was holding onto the side of it, just keeping her head above the waves. She didn't mind the battering, she was just grateful that they let her stay there.

As the weeks went by, Mandy felt more at ease with both girls although she always liked Tina the best. Because she lived closer to Tina she was able to spend that bit more time with her. Petra wasn't always around. She took days off school and she occasionally went to meet her dad's girlfriend to go shopping. Some nights, after her tea, Mandy would wander along to Tina's and ask her if she'd like to come over to her house. Sometimes she did, but she made Mandy promise never to tell Petra and Mandy kept her mouth shut. But as time went on Petra allowed her to do more with The Red Roses and she came to Mandy's house for a sleepover. Mandy even tried to seem interested in Petra's fascination for the rundown house that she was sure was haunted. Mandy had reluctantly followed

Petra and Tina into the back garden of the house one day only to be chased out by an irate next-door neighbour. Sometimes she asked Tina why Petra was so awkward but Tina would never talk about her so Mandy left it.

In the half-term holidays Petra seemed to change. She lost her phone. She was jumpy and didn't seem to care about The Red Roses as much. Her clothes were grotty and she was constantly patting her pocket for the phone that wasn't there. During that half-term week she wore the same top three days running. She looked grubby. When Mandy went to call for Tina she heard her mother asking her, 'What's up with Petra? Is her dad playing up?' And Mandy asked Tina what her mum had meant.

'Petra's dad is sick with alcohol,' she'd said. Mandy had thought she'd meant that Petra's dad had a hangover, but later she learnt that Petra's dad had serious problems with alcohol, that he drank it all day long and sometimes couldn't get out of bed. Petra's mood worsened and she would stand gazing at the old house whenever they went into the newsagent's.

Tina had her own problems during those weeks. Her mum wouldn't allow her to go and stay with her dad and his beautician girlfriend at his South London flat. She had to depend on him visiting and sometimes he said he'd come but didn't and blamed the traffic in the Blackwall Tunnel. Tina's eyes would glisten with tears and Mandy tried to comfort her. She loved those times when it was just the two of them, her and Tina. At night, in bed, Mandy would fantasise that Petra had been run over by a car and killed and that she and Tina were best friends. When they first disappeared it'd made her feel uneasy. It was as if some evil fairy godmother had tuned into her wishes and punished her by getting rid of Petra *and* Tina.

On that Thursday they'd been in Tina's house all afternoon. It was the last but one day of the half-term holidays. They were talking about what they were going to do for Halloween. Mandy's mum and dad were having a party for their friends and had invited Tina and Petra to come and stay over. They were talking about it and deciding whether it would be a good idea if The Red Roses sang a couple of their songs.

Petra stood up suddenly. 'I'm sick of all this, let's go to the shop,' she said, pulling some money out of her pocket.

They'd got to the shop in Princess Street and were about to go in when Petra's attention was taken by the house opposite. Mandy had looked at it then. It was five thirty and it was dark. The house itself was gloomy except for a light in the front ground-floor room. Petra seemed to stare for a long time. Mandy expected her to repeat her usual comment about them going in one day but she put her money away in her pocket and said, 'I think we should go into the old house. We've been talking about it for weeks. There's a key round the back on a hook by the door.'

This was news to Mandy. She'd never heard Petra talk about a *key* before.

In the end, Tina had gone with Petra. Of course she had, she was her best friend. Petra reached across and took Tina's hand. 'Me and Tina always do stuff together. We've been friends for six years. You don't have to come if you don't want to, Mandy. I understand.' And Tina allowed herself to be pulled away into the garden.

Mandy had watched them go with mounting frustration. What was it about that house? It was almost dark, cold; Tina was wearing her mum's hoodie and she pulled the hood up. When the garden gate shut Mandy turned away and felt her temper rise. She was not going to stand around and wait for them! She walked towards home, a feeling of misery hardening inside her. Maybe she should find other friends. Make a new start on Monday, sit with some other kids. She didn't need to be treated like an idiot. The Red Roses was a stupid name for a girl group.

When the news came that neither Petra nor Tina had returned home that evening, Mandy went into a silent panic. 'Do you know where they went?' her mother had asked.

She shook her head vehemently. 'We had a row outside the shop and I came home.' How could she tell her mother that they had gone into the old house and that she may well have gone with them? How could she admit that they had talked about something like that? Then it would come out that they'd gone into the garden once, a couple of weeks before. They'd trespassed and been chased out by a neighbour. That would mean the end of the freedom she had won since going to secondary school. Being allowed to go to Tina's on her own. Having the right to say, 'I'm just going out with Tina and Petra for a while.' Once she'd explained about the house in Princess Street that would all be finished. Then it wouldn't matter that she had no friends because she wouldn't be allowed to go out anyway.

The evening they had disappeared, she had sat on the armchair in the living room watching programmes, flicking the telly from channel to channel while listening to her mum on the phone to other people. One of them was Tina's mum she was sure. There was a charge in the air, adult anxieties that could turn into anger at any moment. Why tell them what had happened when it was most likely that Tina and Petra had *gone on* somewhere. Maybe Petra had taken Tina off with her to do some shopping with her dad's girlfriend? Maybe they had gone for a McDonald's and just forgot to let anyone know. Maybe Tina or Petra had fallen over, twisted an ankle and they were sitting somewhere in A & E. Why mention the house and the reclusive old man who lived there?

But the hours went by and Mandy felt as if her story had pinned her to the spot. When eight o'clock came she couldn't suddenly say, 'Oh, actually, I do know where they went.' Then she heard her mum tell her dad that Alison Pointer was going over to South London to check that Tina hadn't gone on a forbidden visit to see her father and his beautician girlfriend.

Mandy relaxed for a while then because that seemed like a good explanation. Tina had certainly been miffed that she hadn't seen her father over half-term. Maybe when they'd got fed up with the house in Princess Street Petra had said, 'Let's go and visit your dad!' Possibly Tina had written a text to her mother to tell her where she was going without knowing that her phone had run out of power at that very moment and the message had never sent.

Later though Mandy found out that Tina's phone was at home on charge. Neither Tina nor Petra had had a mobile phone with them.

The police came to her house and the television had to be turned off.

There was one question after another.

At eleven o'clock that night she told them the truth.

It suddenly came out. 'I do know where they went,' she said, amid sobs and told them. She watched her mum's face screw up with amazement. The policeman's expression changed instantly. He stood up and sat down again. He got out his phone and spoke into it rapidly, his words sliding together so that she could hardly make out what he was saying. Then he left and her mum and dad stayed on the sofa holding each other's hands, looking at her as if she were a stranger.

Many people had asked Mandy afterwards why she'd not told them at first where the girls had gone. Officer Farraday had sat on the sofa in her front room, his eyes darkened with sadness, and said, 'Why didn't you tell us straight away, Mandy? If we'd known they were in the house we could have gone there immediately. We might have saved them.'

Why hadn't she told them?

Now Mandy picked up her laptop. She clicked on Google and looked up the Safe and Sound website. She opened it up and went on the page that said 'Petra Armstrong'. On one side of the page was a photo of Petra when she was twelve. On the other was the computer-generated image of what Petra would look like if she was seventeen years old. The picture of the older girl was striking. The same long hair was there, the same secretive expression. The face was thinner though and the eyes seemed bigger, although looking closer Mandy thought she could see eye make-up there. The mouth was not quite so sulky, but it wasn't smiling.

Petra Armstrong, almost certainly dead.

Mandy saw her clothes hanging on the wardrobe door. The black jeans hung slim and long from beneath the red top. The high heels sat on the carpet underneath. It wasn't so different from the outfits that Petra and Tina had worn for their girl band. Mandy felt a moment's hurt as she looked at the clothes waiting to be worn. She had never been allowed to join The Red Roses.

Mandy stood up and plucked the hanger from the outside of her wardrobe. She opened the door and slid it in between other garments. She picked the shoes up and placed them on the shelf below. Red was a good colour for her and there was no reason why she should feel bad about it.

Alison had said she didn't blame her any more. Mandy didn't quite believe it. Alison had said it when she was dressed up and holding her sharp and important leather handbag. Then she seemed hard and fortified, that she could forgive anything. Mandy was sure though that when the smart clothes came off and Alison was sitting in her dressing gown and slippers she probably asked herself over and over why Mandy hadn't told anyone where the girls had gone for five hours.

Five hours that could have changed everything.

Eight

The party was due to start at nine. She'd been going to meet Tommy early at a coffee bar on the high street but he'd texted her to say that he had something to do first and would see her at Zoe's house. That meant that she would have to go alone. She hesitated, wondering what to do. There were some other girls that she could meet up with but she didn't want to.

She didn't really have any girl friends in the sixth form. Her closest friend had been Sophie Brewer but her parents had moved house just after Christmas and Sophie was now at a school in Barnet. At first Mandy had kept in touch with her, talking for ages on the phone or sending a stream of emails letting her know what was going on in school. She'd stayed at her new house for a couple of weekends and Sophie had shown her around her new neighbourhood. The contact had lessened though as the months went by. They'd met in Oxford Street a few times for shopping trips but Sophie's stories about her new school and her new friends made Mandy feel left out. She began to make excuses. The contact waned and by the summer holidays she realised that she hadn't sent a text or email or rung Sophie for weeks. She'd not even bothered to look at her Facebook page.

There were friendly girls in school and she often sat with groups that she'd known over the years. It was easy to slip in and out of these relationships as it suited her. When she thought about it, her friendship with Sophie had been a bit like that anyway. Sophie had two younger sisters and a lot of her time was taken up with family stuff. Mandy's friendship with her had always come second place to the things she did in her family. Mandy didn't mind. She often looked round at girls in class who were panicking at the thought of spending a lesson apart from their friend and she sneered. It was better to be self-contained. She could find friendship when she needed it. That way there were no emotional demands made on her.

She decided to go to Zoe's party on her own. She spent a while looking critically at the top and jeans that she'd bought. She tried them on and walked up and down her room in the high heels and realised, with a sinking heart, that these were probably the kind of clothes that Tommy would hate. High street garments that were no doubt made in third-world countries. On top of that they were someone else's style. Tommy would see all that in a moment, even though he'd be too good mannered to say it to her.

She sat down on the corner of her bed. In the shop she'd been carried away with thinking how good the red looked against her skin and that the black jeans made her legs look long. Then there were the shoes. She didn't usually wear heels but these caught her eye. There'd been loud music playing in the shop and the assistant had said that all the girls who worked there had bought a pair of these. So in a moment's extravagance she'd decided to have them.

She should have gone to a charity shop.

Then she wondered if she could say that she'd got these from a charity shop. She held one up in the air. The red leather was pristine. She would need to scuff them up a bit to make it look as though they'd been worn by someone else, if only for a short time. 'Look at this, I picked them up for half nothing,' she would say and Tommy would think that was good because she was recycling something.

The jeans were plain enough. She could wear a black top over them. She could add her home-made jewellery. This was one thing that Tommy approved of about her. He loved that she made these bracelets and necklaces. He always commented on them and said that it was important to make our own things and not always rely on other people to manufacture them for us.

He thought a lot about the planet and resources.

She'd never known a boy like him before. That was why she had such strong feelings for him. Maybe, tonight, at the party, she could let him know in some way. There would be alcohol and it was always forgivable to do outrageous things when drunk. If she misjudged it then she could always say, 'Oh, don't mind me! I always get emotional when I'm drunk. You didn't think I meant it, did you?'

She got dressed and put her beads on. Her mother was downstairs fidgeting with a duster in the hallway. She put on her coat.

'What time shall Dad pick you up?' her mother said.

'I hate saying a time,' Mandy said. 'Can't I just get a cab?'

'He doesn't mind staying up late. What time? Twelve? One?'

'Can I just ring? I won't be later than one. I promise.'

'OK, I'll tell Dad.'

Mandy walked round her.

'Are those shoes new?' her mother said.

'Charity shop,' Mandy said, trying on the lie to see how it sounded.

The party was crowded when she got there. She said hello to the kids she knew and Zoe took her to the kitchen area. She kept her coat on, not sure where to put it. Zoe pointed out her brothers and their mates. Then the bell rang and she left Mandy alone. Zoe's brothers were taller and broader than most of the kids there and they had more hair on their faces. Mandy walked round them and headed for the table of drinks. She put down a bottle of wine and then looked for a can of beer. The room was semi-dark but someone had strung fairy lights across the cupboard doors. It looked welcoming, like Christmas. She began to relax.

She looked around to see who'd just come in. Her eye scanned the room, looking for Tommy. But it wasn't him; just some kids she didn't know.

'Are you not staying?' a voice said.

It was a Lucy, a girl from her history group. Mandy hardly knew her. She was pointing at her coat.

'I'm feeling a bit cold,' she said, not wanting to take it off yet.

'How are you finding history? I wish the teacher would stop lecturing. I get so bored.'

'Yeah.'

Actually Mandy didn't get bored in history but that was because she was sitting beside Tommy. He kept her entertained. She thought it might be dreary otherwise.

'What are you doing in English? I'm in the parallel group.'

Mandy screwed her face up, trying to think. She'd never spoken to Lucy before. She wondered why the girl had struck up this conversation.

'I think we're doing *Cat on a Hot Tin Roof*.'

'I wish we were! We're starting *Antony and Cleopatra* after half-term!'

People were trying to get past them to get to the drinks. Mandy was moving here and there and couldn't quite hear Lucy.

'Do you want to come into the other room? There's more space,' Lucy said, in a louder voice.

'Sure.'

She followed her out, looking around all the time in case Tommy had come and she had missed him. The living room was bigger and some people were sitting down on the sofa. The music was loud but no one was dancing. Lucy headed over to the window. Mandy noticed that she had really long hair. It had wispy ends like baby hair and Mandy wondered if she was one of those girls who'd never had a haircut.

She was feeling very hot in her coat. She shrugged her shoulders at Lucy and took it off.

'Warm in here . . .' she said.

'Put it over there,' Lucy said, pointing to a chair in the corner that had coats draped over it.

After she left her coat she stood by Lucy and kept her eye on the window where she could see the front garden and the path. When Tommy came she would see him.

'I love your beads and bangles. You make them, don't you? I heard you saying one day. I always wondered why you didn't do matching earrings.'

'That's a bit too technical for me. I collect nice and unusual beads. I can string them but I haven't mastered anything as clever as earrings.'

'My mum could show you. She makes earrings and sells them on a market stall. My mum made these!'

Lucy pulled her hair back and showed off a beaded earring. It was striking: long and colourful. A little wasted hidden behind Lucy's heavy hair.

'They're really pretty.'

'My mum's really artistic. I'm the opposite. All I seem to do is study. I want to go to Oxford. So I have to get high grades. Are you planning to go to uni?'

'I might. I haven't thought that far ahead.'

'Oh you need to. Do some research on universities. There are some good ones and some terrible ones. You don't want to waste your student loan.'

The music had stopped and there were a few moments of silence. Mandy gazed out of the window. She saw Tommy come up the front path of the house. She stood up straight. He was here. She felt herself smiling. Lucy must have noticed the difference in Mandy because she looked out of the window as well.

'I really like Tommy,' Lucy said, 'don't you? He's so different from the other guys, so easy to talk to.'

Mandy nodded, looking down at the red shoes, wondering whether she should have worn them or not.

'I was surprised about him and Leanne getting together!'

'What?'

'Tommy and Leanne. They've been seeing each other. I saw them after school yesterday afternoon. I had a tutorial with my English teacher and I was leaving late and I saw them holding hands.'

'Leanne?'

Mandy was touching the beads on her necklace, spinning them.

'I was amazed. I knew he was always hanging out with Toni and Leanne but I guess I thought it was Toni he liked. She seems much more like him. You know, a bit zany in the way she dresses. But Leanne?'

Mandy felt herself weaken. Her shoes seemed higher all of a sudden and she felt she might topple off them. She looked for somewhere to put her beer can.

'Are you OK?' Lucy said.

The front door bell rang. Tommy was coming in and Mandy couldn't face him. *Leanne?* He was with *Leanne?*

'I just . . .'

Lucy's face changed. She frowned and seemed to squeeze her lips together.

'You didn't know.'

Mandy stood back, behind the living room door, and Lucy moved to stay with her. The music was louder and a couple of girls were dancing, which made the living room look crowded. From behind the door Mandy could hear the sound of Tommy's voice. Was Leanne with him? That was something she couldn't face. Lucy was staring at her with concern.

'You like him, don't you? I didn't realise. I just thought you were mates. I'm really sorry I said anything.'

Tommy didn't come into the living room and Mandy knew he must have gone straight towards the kitchen like most of the partygoers, heading for the table with the drinks.

'Can you get my coat for me?' she said.

'Oh, don't go. There are lots of guys here . . .'

'Please.'

Lucy seemed to think for a moment, then she strode across the room, and sorted out Mandy's coat.

'Thanks,' Mandy said, putting it on. 'If anyone asks, just say I didn't feel very well.'

'Sure. Will you be all right?'

Mandy walked out of the living room, leaving the music behind, and went through the front door as a group of kids came in. No one noticed her; no one said anything. It was like she was invisible. As if she'd never gone to the party at all.

Nine

She walked home. She didn't call her dad but made her own way back. She trudged through the streets by herself for almost an hour. She thought about the party and felt wave after wave of embarrassment. She'd not been there for longer than thirty minutes. Maybe she should have stayed, seen Tommy, made a show of pretending that everything was normal. And if Leanne had been there she could have chatted and said, 'How did you and Tommy get together?' As if it were no big deal. As if it were something she might have expected.

During the walk she felt a choking hurt that clenched her chest. Getting further away from the party it seemed to loosen just a little and she just experienced a kind of disbelief that she'd ever thought that there might be something between her and Tommy. He'd been sweet and attentive and always keen to spend time with her but it'd never been anything to do with *attraction*. She was his mate. That was all. No one else thought they might be paired off because Lucy had told her about Leanne without flinching, with no sense that it might offend or upset Mandy. She had never considered Mandy as girlfriend material for Tommy and hadn't thought, for a second, that Mandy had that idea either.

It was probably the same for everyone else in the sixth form.

She was the only person who hadn't known. She felt tears in her eyes at this thought. It was *shameful* that she hadn't realised. Was she some kind of idiot? Maybe if she hadn't been so wound up with all this other stuff about Petra and Tina. If she'd not had that on her mind she might have looked calmly round the common room and seen the signs that Tommy was attracted to Leanne and then realised in time, before she made an emotional show of herself in front of Lucy.

Her head was filled up with what happened years before. She was so preoccupied she couldn't see what was going on under her own nose, she couldn't think straight, otherwise she would have realised that Tommy wasn't for her. He was interesting, full of ideas, funny, good company. Why would he want her?

She got home and avoided questions about the party and why she hadn't called for a lift. Her dad was tired and yawned his way up the stairs to his room. She went straight to bed and seemed to fall asleep quickly.

She woke up just after three. She tried to go back to sleep but was still tossing and turning an hour later. Eventually she sat up. Her room felt cold. She put her bedside light on and took a drink from the glass of water beside her. She looked over at her wardrobe. Her red top was still hanging on the outside of the door. She hadn't even worn it. It hung there like a flag that had been lowered.

She shouldn't have gone to the party at all. She should have stayed at home and wallowed in the thoughts that had been weighing her head down this week. She got up. She walked to the window and pulled the curtain back a few centimetres and looked out. It was black and there was mist or possibly fog. She could see it making the street light hazy.

She wondered about the house on Princess Street. She hadn't passed by it since Tuesday morning when the bulldozers were starting up. Alison Pointer said that it'd been almost flattened. Mandy tried to picture what it looked like. There would be a big gap and the walls of the adjacent houses would look odd and exposed. You would be able to look straight through to what had been the back garden. She wondered if the demolishers had taken the trees and bushes as well. There'd been a lot of them she remembered from years before but they may have been cleared by the people who lived in the flats. There'd been brick sheds at the bottom of the garden too. Had they been flattened?

It was twenty past four and she was wide awake. Her mum and dad wouldn't get up for hours. It felt freezing, and the heating wasn't due to come on until seven. The silence of the house seemed to stifle her. She felt restless and wanted to go out, *do something*. Later, maybe after lunch, she could go on Facebook and congratulate Tommy on getting together with Leanne. That would be an easy way of getting over the awkward embarrassment of being told about it. She could ask Tommy what had gone on at the party, who was wearing what, who got drunk, and so on. It would be just as if nothing unusual had happened.

There was a tightness in her throat at the thought of Tommy and Leanne being together. Leanne wasn't his kind of girl at all. Leanne was an identikit teenage girl, one of the many in school who looked similar, talked about the same things, wore the same clothes. Mandy couldn't think of a single time that she'd said something interesting in class or socially. Leanne was pretty, and wore lots of make-up. Her clothes were tight and always showed the outline of her breasts and her slim hips. Leanne didn't wear charity shop clothes and didn't care about things like recycling. Whenever Mandy saw her in the toilets she was layering lipstick on her mouth and smacking her lips together, eyeing herself in the mirror to make sure she looked good.

Leanne was *not* the girl for Tommy, she thought miserably.

The whole of Sunday stretched ahead of her. How would she get through it?

She made a decision. She pulled her nightclothes off and put on her jeans and jumper. She slipped into her boots and got a jacket out. She picked up her phone and then left her room, creeping along the landing and tiptoeing quietly downstairs. There was no sound at all from her parents' room. They were fast asleep. She picked up her key from the hall table and then unhooked the chain on the front door and opened it, turning the lock slowly. She stepped out into the early morning. The mist seemed as though it were clinging to the street lights. She had the key in the lock so that she could turn it as the door closed to avoid any noise. Once it was shut she stood there for a few moments, tensing herself in case a light at the top of the stairs flickered on and her mother came running down. The house remained silent, so she walked on up the street. As she went her eyes grew accustomed to the dark.

It took less than five minutes to get to Princess Street. The roads were hushed, with just a single cyclist in a fluorescent jacket. The newsagent's was shut. She crossed over to the other side and soon saw the place where the house had been.

A car passed slowly behind her and its headlights lit up the area for a few seconds. The space between the buildings was wide and long. She could see how the owners had got permission for a block of apartments. There was a wire fence across the front and she walked up to it. She frowned when she saw that it'd been pulled away at the side, vandalised already. She stood staring through it and her eyes began to pick out shapes. Two huge trees towering at the back. It looked as though most of the garden had been flattened. Maybe it would become a car park for the tenants.

She looked at the place where the wire had been pulled away from the post. The very bottom of it had curled back on itself. Then she glanced up and down the road. The street lamps were yellow, the mist eddying round the light. A car passed by, slowing down to go over a hump. She wondered who was up so early on a Sunday morning.

She pulled at the loose wire. It came away up to her waist. Then she crouched down on her knees, edged through the gap and stood up quickly on the other side, brushing the dirt from her jeans. She walked over to the wall of one of the adjacent houses and then stood against it so that she wasn't visible to anyone passing by. From where she was standing she could see the ground that had been under the house. There was a faint outline of bricks, as if someone had drawn a line round the outside wall of what had been the house. Inside the line there was some concrete and earth in places and some slabs of stone sticking up. The area at the back, which had once been the garden, was mostly dug over and looked soft and mulchy. The brick sheds at the back were gone and just the two trees were left standing, looking lonely and out of place.

She edged along the wall until she came to the end of the neighbouring house. The garden fence was high and solid so she walked beside it until she came to the far corner of the garden. She stood in it and looked towards the road. She had seen the house from that position before. She remembered standing there and looking at it on the day that Petra had led them into the garden.

It was an inset training day and they'd been off school. It had been hot, an autumn day that still felt like summer. Petra had made a sudden decision that they should go in. Then she'd said, 'I dare you!' and made Tina say it back to her. Mandy had been baffled. What was the point? But Petra and Tina had marched off and she didn't want to be left behind. She'd followed them into the front garden and then round the side through a gate. They'd emerged into a big overgrown garden. There was a narrow path round the side of the building that led to the back door. The rest of the garden was uncared for, the grass half a metre high, the bushes thick, their foliage reaching out and throwing everything into shade. Mandy could see a couple of white brick sheds. She'd headed towards it and was pleased when Tina followed her. They were only there for moments it seemed when the neighbour appeared. His face had loomed up from behind a bush in the next garden and had given Mandy a start. He wore heavy black glasses and he'd shouted loudly at them. She'd rushed back down the garden, flattening the grass as she went towards the side gate. Tina had followed. Once out, they'd run all the way along the street until they got to the next corner and then they'd stopped, out of breath, Mandy bending over, holding a stitch in her side, Tina looking startled. Then Petra came tearing round the corner and somehow the three of them had started laughing.

Mandy looked hard into the darkness of the garden. She could see the detritus left over by the demolishers. There was a wheelbarrow that had fallen to one side, looking as though it belonged to the old house rather than the workmen. Near where the sheds had been there was a jumble of terracotta pots. There were small piles of bricks scattered around, as if thrown carelessly about.

Just then a car pulled up, slowing right down on the street.

Mandy focused on it, tried to make out what colour it was and who was in it. It came to a stop and she felt immediately tense. She wasn't supposed to be there. A dreadful thought occurred to her. What if it was someone from the party? She moved sideways until she was standing behind the trunk of one of the big trees. The car sat there for a few moments and Mandy could hear sounds coming from inside it: the heater, the radio, the engine running. Then the driver must have turned the key because it all stopped and the car was silent and still. There were people inside but Mandy couldn't see them and she couldn't tell what kind of car it was. Still no one moved. She felt a growing sense of panic. Could it be the people from the demolition company? Had someone come to fix the fence? But at five o'clock in the morning? Was it a security firm? Either way, she couldn't be caught there. What kind of story would that be for people: after all this time and everything bad that had happened in this house Mandy Crystal *still* couldn't stay away. What would people say? Her mother? Alison Pointer? Dr Shukla?

She looked hopelessly around. The garden fences were solid. The houses on each side were in complete darkness. She couldn't slip away into some alley that ran along the back because there wasn't one.

The car sat there silent. Then the passenger's door opened. No one got out. It hung there for a few moments and then a pair of legs came into view.

Mandy moved further behind the tree, feeling the rough bark on the side of her face. She peeked round. A young woman emerged. She stood up and closed the door of the car quietly, the *click* barely sounding. She walked towards the fence carrying a torch. Mandy could see the beam pointing out in a straight line. She came up to the edge of the property. Mandy felt her shoulders knotting. It *was* something to do with this house and Mandy was stuck where she couldn't get out. Maybe the woman was from a security company, called out by some electronic alarm that Mandy had stumbled over. That was why she was wearing normal clothes: she wasn't in uniform, she was *on call*.

The torch sent a finger of light onto the site. The mist swirled through it. The beam was strong where the woman was but then fanned out and faded as it swept the back of the garden. The woman swung the torch from one side to the other, slowly as if she was looking for something. Was she searching for an intruder?

She turned it off and the place seemed darker than it had been before.

The woman stood looking at the site. Then she fiddled with the torch so that it lit up for a split second and illuminated her face.

Mandy stared. The light went off but she'd already seen the girl's face, bright white, in the light from the torch. She came out from behind the tree. She walked a few paces. The girl was still there and she'd turned the torch on again. It pointed into the centre of the garden, the place where the house would have been. The girl hadn't noticed her because she was outside the light, but Mandy found herself drawn by the brightness, moving closer to the beam that cut through the old property. When she was a few metres away, the girl saw her and jumped. She snapped the torch off.

'Petra,' Mandy said, her voice hoarse, stuck down her throat. 'Petra, it's me, Mandy.

The girl looked stunned, horrified. Behind her the car started up. The noise made Mandy start. The girl turned and headed back to the car.

'Petra,' Mandy called out. 'Wait!'

But the car was moving off at speed. In seconds it was gone. Mandy got down on her knees and scrambled under the wire. When she stood up in the street she saw the taillights of the car turning the corner.

It was gone.

Ten

Miss Pearce and Tommy seemed busy preparing for the memorial most of the afternoon. The sixth-form common room was closed off and the only place to sit in-between lessons was the lunch area, which was still grubby from lunchtime and smelt of chips. Mandy had a free period after English so she sat at a table as far away from the serving area as she could. Some other sixth formers were there as well. They were still talking about Zoe's party. The ripple of conversation had been there all day. Zoe's older brothers had kept things under control so, although there had been alcohol and dope and loud music, it'd never got out of hand. There had been no fights and no gatecrashers but there had been plenty of drunkenness and lots of people getting together. No one said anything about Tommy and Leanne. Maybe no one wanted to say anything within Mandy's earshot. Maybe they all knew that she had feelings for Tommy. How could they not? She'd been following him round for weeks.

Not that any of it really mattered. Not with what she'd had in her head since early yesterday morning. She was still in a state of shock. That was the only way she could explain the numbness inside her. She had seen Petra Armstrong. *Hadn't she?* She had stood on that demolition site and watched seventeen-year-old Petra get out of a car, walk up to the fence and use a torch to look around the remnants of the old house that she'd once been fixated on.

Or had Mandy been mistaken? She'd spent the week thinking about that time five years ago, and then she'd looked at Alison Pointer's website and the computer-generated image of what Petra looked like now. She'd had Petra on her mind ever since the house had been demolished. Maybe she'd *wanted* to see Petra there and had conjured her up, superimposed her face onto that of the security woman who'd been on call and was checking the site for vandalism.

So why, when Mandy called out to her, had she not stood her ground, ordered Mandy out of the site, taken her name and address or called the police and had her charged with trespassing? Why had she turned tail, scuttled off into the car and driven away at speed?

She remembered the moment that she'd seen Petra's face. The torch had lit it up for a second and the skin had been ghostly white. But she'd had a moment's recognition. In that expression she'd seen the twelve-year-old Petra. The blank stare and the lips puckered suspiciously to one side. It had been *her*, she was sure. But was it just like the bus sightings? She'd been sure each of those times as well.

Twice she'd been in that garden. The first time she'd been chased out by the angry neighbour. A glimpse of his face flashed through her head and she remembered something that she hadn't thought about for years. The week after the three of them had crept into the garden she'd seen the neighbour again. He'd been in front of Mandy and her mum in the supermarket. She'd been unloading the shopping onto the conveyor belt and he'd stared at her for a moment and then she'd realised who he was. She felt herself go red and could feel his eyes on her and she rearranged the tins and bottles so that they went through first. 'Heaviest stuff at the bottom,' she'd whispered to no one in particular and then told her mum she wanted to look at the magazines. She walked off, her face burning, and anxiously hung round the books and magazines, thinking that the man would tell her mum what she'd done. But moments later she saw her mum pushing the trolley towards her. She was smiling at something so Mandy knew he hadn't said anything.

She looked round and saw that Tommy had come into the hall. She shrunk a little in her seat because she sensed that he was looking for her. Something to do with the memorial service, no doubt. The very thought of it made her shoulders stiffen. He saw her then and waved, and came walking across, full of purpose, intent on speaking to her. A renewed sense of sadness hit her. A little bit of her had thought that his interest in the service had been because he was interested in *her*, but now she realised that wasn't true. This was a project for him, like all the other things he did.

'Hi!' he said breathlessly. 'I wondered if you'd come along to the common room so that I could just go through things with you. Just to check that you think it's OK?'

'Sure,' she said, getting up, pushing her empty paper cup away.

She followed him along the corridor as he talked about the memorial. He was having music and poems and a couple of spots where teachers would say a few things about their memories of Petra and Tina and then he was going to say something about loss. He was ticking the sections off on his fingers in a businesslike way and she wondered if he would put this on his CV. But then she felt bad. He wasn't someone who just did things for show; he did things because he liked them. She was allowing her disappointment to turn into something nasty and spiteful.

She'd seen him with Leanne first thing that morning and it hadn't been awkward. Mandy had simply said, 'Hello! I heard about you two guys!' with as much nonchalance as she could manage. The rest of the morning had been busy and the twisty feeling she had in her chest seemed to uncurl. After the memorial school would go back to normal and then it would be half-term. After the holidays she could disentangle herself from the group and put some space between herself and Tommy.

The common room had been set out with chairs and a small platform. Behind it was a whiteboard with an open laptop on a small table beside it. Tommy ducked around the chairs and went up onto the platform. He leant over the laptop and pressed a couple of buttons and the white screen was filled with two photographs of Petra and Tina. They weren't official school photos although Petra was wearing a school uniform in hers. She'd been in a group but the others had been cut out and Mandy wondered if it'd been taken on the day their class had gone on the museum trip. The photo of Tina was quite different. She was standing outside a front door, possibly her own, and she was wearing a dress and boots and a loose cardigan. Her hands were clasped as if she didn't quite know what to do with them.

'So, we're starting with this music,' Tommy said.

A snatch of music came on. It was orchestral, sombre. Mandy recognised a cello playing. The tune was familiar, something she'd heard in the past, but she couldn't have named it.

'Then we are going to have the teachers' memories and then this.'

A song came on which Mandy recognised instantly. It was one of the songs that'd been very popular when they'd been friends. The girls had practised it over and over.

'Tina Pointer's mother gave me this. She said that Tina and Petra used to sing this as a girl band.'

Mandy heard it play and immediately pictured Petra singing and Tina backing her up. Once, just once, Mandy had suggested that maybe two back-up singers would have been better than one. Petra told her, in a firm tone, that it was a duo, a *two*-girl group.

'The Red Roses, they were called,' he said.

'I know what they were called, Tommy. I was friends with them.'

'Course you were. Sorry, that must have sounded completely dumb!'

'Did Miss Pearce say why we're having this now? The anniversary is on the twenty-eighth and it's only the nineteenth.'

'Yeah, course. The twenty-eighth is in half-term and she wanted to get this done so that the rest of the week was clear.'

'She wanted to get it out of the way?'

'No! I didn't mean that. It's just that there are other more upbeat things that are planned and it seemed a good idea to . . .'

'Get it done.'

Tommy looked awkward. She tried to be positive.

'I understand. It's best this way,' she said in a faux-cheerful voice. 'Anyway, I should be off. What time does it start?'

'Last period has been suspended for the lower sixth. So we'll begin about three. In about twenty minutes?'

'OK,' Mandy said, her cheeks feeling tired from holding a smile.

She left the common room and walked swiftly away, not quite knowing where she was headed. She knew for sure she didn't want to go to the memorial. She had no wish to sit through another ceremony in memory of Tina and Petra, especially one organised by Tommy. The buzzer went for the end of lesson. The noise increased as students spilt out onto the corridors, calling to each other and letting doors bang behind them. Mandy kept walking towards the reception area where it was quieter and calmer. Being a sixth former meant she didn't have to sign out so she went straight for the doors.

Before she got there she heard someone call her name. She closed her eyes with annoyance. She didn't want to go back and sit through Tommy's ceremony. She stopped and turned round. It was Jon Wallis. He was walking towards her. He smiled and patted his pocket. He pulled something out of it.

'I've been looking for you,' he said.

He held out an envelope to her.

'At lunchtime a girl gave me this. She was outside school and she asked me if I knew you and told me to give this to you.'

'At lunchtime?' she said, puzzled.

'I looked for you but the common room was being used and then I had a class.'

She took the envelope. Her name was written on the front of it: 'Mandy Crystal'.

'Thanks,' she said.

'You're not going to the memorial?' Jon said.

She shook her head.

'I don't blame you. Pointless exercise.'

He walked away and she pulled the envelope open. Inside was a postcard with some handwriting on it.

Please don't tell anyone that you saw me.
I will contact you.

The handwriting was untidy as if it'd been done in a hurry. She read it again and then the meaning sunk in. There was no signature but she knew who it was from. She turned it over as if there might be more information on the other side, but it was a picture. A picture postcard, the kind you pin on a board. The image seemed to jump out at her then. It wasn't just any floral design. It was a photograph of a bunch of red roses.

The Red Roses. It was just a duo and Mandy had never been allowed to join.

Petra had contacted her.

PART TWO: The Past

Petra

Eleven

It was Petra's twelfth birthday. Three cards stood on the table: one from her dad, one from Zofia – his girlfriend – and one from Tina. In her bag there was a card from Mandy, the new girl at school, but she hadn't taken it out of the envelope yet.

It was gone five and she was ironing a shirt for her dad. She could hear him in his bedroom singing along with the radio. He was picking up an airport fare that evening and wanted to look smart. Petra took care that the iron was not too hot. Her dad was particular about his clothes. Hanging on the back of the door was his best jacket, still covered with the dry cleaner's plastic bag. Petra had picked it up on her way home from school. She'd already removed the laundry tag from the inside pocket but she'd left it covered because her dad liked it like that.

Her phone beeped. She took it out of her pocket. There was a message from Zofia:

Happy Birthday Kochanie ☺

She grinned. Zofia was always using Polish words. *Kochanie* meant 'honey' or 'baby'. Zofia was very affectionate.

Petra turned the iron off. In her back pocket there were two twenty pound notes: her birthday present from her dad. She still had other gifts to look forward to: Tina's and Zofia's. Tina said that her mum, Mrs Pointer, had something small for her too. She was going there for her tea and a sleepover as soon as she'd got changed.

Her dad came into the living room. He was wearing black trousers and a white short-sleeved vest. He was singing along to the music that was still playing from his bedroom. His hands were in tiny fists in front of his chest, moving like pistons in time with the beat. He closed his eyes and exaggerated the movements as if he were at a disco. She shook her head. He had good rhythm, she had to admit, but his way of dancing was embarrassingly old fashioned.

The track ended and he opened his eyes. He was threading his new leather belt through the loops on his trousers. When he had done up the buckle she handed him the ironed shirt, which was still warm. He slipped his arms into it and began buttoning it up. He was humming something all the while. She scooped up a tie from the back of the settee and held it up.

'Good girl, Petra,' he said, taking it and draping it around his neck. 'You want a lift to your friend's house? I can go that way.'

She shook her head as he concentrated on the tie, knotting it but leaving it loose at his neck, like lots of the boys in school did. He picked up his jacket and unpeeled the plastic wrapping. Then he put it on, brushing it down.

'How do I look?' he said.

'Good. Who are you picking up?'

'New client, Mr Constantine. Off the books so no tax. A mate gave him my name. I'm meeting him at Heathrow then he wants me to drive him round a number of places in the West End.'

'Like a chauffeur?'

'Kind of. It might become a regular thing. Give me a bit of cash in the bank. It's better than just taking people to hospital and back day after day! You'll be OK? Round your friend's? I won't be back till morning.'

'Course.'

He picked up his phone from the table.

'Listen to this,' he said and held it out in the air.

A ringtone sounded. It was the theme tune of a television programme. Petra smiled. Her dad was always getting new ringtones and playing them to her.

'Cool, isn't it?'

'It's all right,' she said, rolling her eyes. No one said 'cool' any more.

He put his phone in his jacket pocket and looked as if he was about to go. He hesitated though and turned back to Petra.

'We're all right, aren't we? You and me? After the other night. No hard feelings?'

Petra frowned. She looked down at the ironing board. The cover was stretched and the thin foam backing was showing through in places. They really needed a new one but they never seemed to get round to buying it.

'I had a few too many; you know that, don't you? I wasn't myself.'

Petra glanced at her forearm. The sleeve of her blouse covered her skin. When she looked up her dad caught her eye. He looked expectant, as though there was some particular thing he was waiting for her to say.

'I know,' she said. 'I understand.'

He stepped across to her, put his arm around her shoulder and gave her a kiss on the head. She could smell his aftershave and feel the heat of his body.

'You get me, Petra, don't you? You know I don't mean any harm,' he said.

'Yes.'

'You're my best girl.'

A music track sounded from the radio in his bedroom and he let go of her. He began to dance backwards, his eyes closed, his fists keeping the beat.

'You should go,' she said. 'You might be late.'

'Chop! Chop! You're right. See you, love!'

When the front door shut, she found herself relaxing. The music was still playing from her dad's bedroom so she walked in and turned the radio off. His room was in disarray, his discarded clothes lying across the bed, his shoes at angles on the floor beside a pair of trainers. She made a *tsking* sound. He liked his things kept in order. She picked up the clothes and put them in the washing basket. Then she tidied the shoes, lining them up along the edge of his wardrobe. She smoothed the duvet and walked across to his window. She put her arm up to draw the curtain. The cuff on her blouse fell back and she saw the bruise then, a splash of navy that would slowly turn yellow and brown. At least her wrist wasn't painful any more.

He hadn't meant to hurt her. He'd just lost his temper.

She closed his bedroom door and felt her spirits rise. There was the sleepover to look forward to.

On the way to Tina's house she thought about The Red Roses. Their performance wasn't as polished as she wanted it to be. And the new girl in school, Mandy, was getting on her nerves, always mooning around. She'd told her, nicely, that she couldn't be in the group and she'd said that was fine, but Petra had seen how enviously she looked at them when they were rehearsing.

The Red Roses had been Petra's idea. She'd decided that she and Tina would form a group. They sang songs at Tina's mum's birthday party. They wore black leggings and red T-shirts and had silk roses in their hair that were fastened onto headbands. They wore deep red lipstick and sang hits from the charts using a karaoke machine.

One day they might go on one of the talent shows on television.

In school they didn't use the machine, just practised their singing and their dance moves and designed costumes for their performances. They intended to ask Miss Pearce if they could perform at a year assembly but not until they were word-perfect and their dances were choreographed. When Mandy started at the school and hung round with them she acted as a kind of audience. They were definitely going to make a short film for YouTube.

Petra turned the corner onto Princess Street. It was still light and there were kids in school uniform hanging around the newsagent's. She looked away as she passed them and crossed the road towards the turning for Tina's street. She sighed as she thought back to Mandy. She didn't *dislike* her, but it was odd having someone new around. Mandy's mother was friendly with Tina's so they couldn't ignore her. But Petra and Tina had been best friends for as long as she could remember. It had always just been the two of them. Now Mandy was always there and it made Petra a little insecure.

Tonight though it was just her and Tina.

She was approaching number fifty-three Princess Street. When Petra was on her own she often slowed down at this garden wall and stared at the house. The place had fascinated her for the last few months, ever since the day her dad had pulled up at it to deliver a package. She'd waited in his cab while he'd gone in the side gate and then come out moments later. Now she came to a complete stop and scrutinised it. The house was bigger and older than all the others in the street and it was crumbling. The brickwork was chipped and battered, and the wood around the windows was fraying, the paintwork peeling off like skin. The solid wood front door had had its corner eaten away by something. The guttering was hanging down and when it was raining a stream of water poured from it.

It was broken down. If it'd been a car it would've been taken to the scrapyard.

No one ever saw the owner. Her dad had told her about him though. His name was Mr Merchant. He knew because he sometimes did errands for him. Mr Merchant was a recluse, which meant he never went out. He was thin, his legs like sticks. He could hardly get off his chair to answer the door. He lived in a room at the front of the house, her dad said. The rest of the place was unused. Every single room had been taken over by cobwebs and if you looked hard enough you could see mice darting in-between the skirting boards.

But that wasn't the worst thing, he said. At times there were mysterious knocking sounds that came from upstairs, even though Mr Merchant clearly lived alone. Once or twice, her dad said, he had glimpsed some shadowy movements in the hallway. One night, after bringing Mr Merchant some shopping, he'd gone up the stairs to check that no one had broken in and had felt something brushing at the back of his neck. He said it'd made his skin crawl.

Petra had shivered at this thought.

She'd pointed it out to Mandy a couple of days ago when they were walking home from school. Mandy had said, 'What a dump!' Petra had been put out by this. That was the trouble with new friends. Their thinking wasn't always the same as yours. *Tina* knew that Petra was interested in this house so she chatted to her about it. Tina understood Petra. One day Petra had told her that the two of them (without Mandy) would creep into the house to have a look around. Tina had made a face at this but Petra wasn't worried. She could always persuade Tina to do the things she wanted her to do.

Later that night, after they'd watched recordings of some *X Factor* and eaten pizza, crisps and ice cream, she suggested to Tina that they should become blood sisters. Tina agreed instantly. Petra explained, solemnly, that Mandy was not to know about it. Tina promised and crossed the fingers on both hands. When it was time for them to go to bed Petra smuggled a knife from Tina's mum's kitchen up to the bedroom. When the house had gone quiet and she was sure Tina's mum was asleep she pulled it out from under her pillow and sliced the top of her thumb with it.

'Oh!' Tina whispered loudly, her face shocked.

Petra moaned quietly as blood oozed from the cut. She held her thumb in the air and ignored the sharp stinging pain that came from it.

'Your turn,' she whispered to Tina, holding the knife out.

Tina looked a bit sick and shook her head rapidly.

'Just a tiny prick.'

'I don't . . . My mum will . . .'

Petra grabbed Tina's thumb and held the point of the knife to her skin. Tina's eyes were tightly closed and she was baring her teeth. Petra felt a moment's hesitation. She'd done it to herself but it was harder to do it to someone else. Especially as she felt Tina pulling her arm back. She glanced at her own thumb now, dripping blood onto her T-shirt. She quickly pushed the point of the blade onto the soft pad of Tina's thumb.

'Ow!'

Tina opened her eyes and saw her blood.

'Quick!'

Petra placed her thumb on top of Tina's. Using her other hand she put pressure on each thumb, pushing them tightly together.

'So that our blood can mingle,' she explained to Tina who was looking queasy.

'Are we blood sisters now?' Tina said.

'For ever,' Petra said.

Tina glanced down at Petra's forearm. The bruise was there: a dark cloud on her skin.

'I knocked into something,' she said, still holding the thumbs together.

Tina averted her eyes. She had seen Petra's bruises before.

The next day, Petra got back to the flat just after two. As soon as she opened the door she saw her dad's keys on the hall table. The place was silent though: no radio, no television. He had gone to bed. In the living room his jacket was draped across the back of the sofa and there was a cup and plate on the coffee table. His bedroom door was shut and from inside she could hear the low sound of snoring.

She dropped her bag and went towards the kitchen. On top of the workshop was a sheet of paper. Her dad's handwriting was scrawled across it.

> Don't cook anything.
> Sophie is bringing a takeaway. Dad.

Her dad insisted on calling his girlfriend 'Sophie'. Zofia was amused by it. 'It's easier for English people to say Sophie.' But Petra liked the polish name: Zofia Banach from Warsaw. Her phone vibrated and she pulled it out of her pocket. It was another text. Perhaps Zofia *sensed* in some way that Petra was thinking of her. She opened it up.

I buy Chinese, moja mała róża, OK? ☺

Moja mała róża was Polish for 'my little rose'. Zofia had started to use it after she'd explained about her and Tina's duo, The Red Roses.

Zofia's texts always made her smile.

Her dad used to smile a lot when he first brought Zofia to the flat, when they started seeing each other. Nowadays, though, he mostly looked serious and sometimes a little irritated by her. Zofia didn't seem to notice. Petra had watched Zofia humming while making her dad a cup of tea and then seen him roll his eyes at something she said. It made her feel sad to see it.

She found herself frowning and used her hand to rub at her wrist, which had started to ache again. She tried to push gloomy thoughts out of her mind. It was her birthday. There was the Chinese to look forward to and Zofia would certainly have bought her a present.

Twelve

Zofia was washing the plates and Petra was drying up. Her dad was watching football on the television in the front room. There was a pile of silver cartons on the worktop that the food had come in. Over one of the chairs was a red nightie that Zofia had bought Petra for her birthday. It was exactly the same shade as the clothes she wore for The Red Roses. In the middle of the table was Zofia's card to Petra. It was pink and had sparkles on it.

From the living room the sound of cheering was loud. It felt like a normal family evening. Petra could imagine Tina standing in her kitchen, drying up the plates for her mum. Tina's dad wouldn't be there of course, he would be in South London with the beautician he'd moved in with some months before. Tina's life would always seem more normal than Petra's though. She wondered, for a second, about Mandy. She lived with her mum and dad, so she was the most *normal* of the three of them.

Petra chewed at the side of her lip. She didn't really like comparing her life to that of other people. She hadn't, not until Mandy had started to hang round with them. Mandy was always so well turned out, her hair neatly brushed and held back with ties. Petra would bet that even her shoes were polished. She

93

always did her homework, had packets of highlighters in her bag and all her books were covered with posh paper.

'What happened, *Anioł?*' Zofia said, touching the plaster on Petra's thumb.

Anioł was the Polish word for 'angel'.

'Cut it on a piece of paper.'

Zofia frowned as if she didn't believe her. They were looking directly at each other because Zofia was small, just a shade taller than Petra. She wore heels all the time and she was always squaring her shoulders and straightening her neck. Her red hair was often up in a ponytail or a bun because it gave her a few more centimetres of height. The nice thing about looking straight at Zofia was that it made it seem as though she was a friend and not a woman who happened to be her dad's girlfriend.

'How is school?'

'OK.'

'And Tina is good?'

'OK. But we've got this other girl who hangs around with us now and she gets on my nerves a bit.'

'Two is good. Three not so good? Too many arguments. My sister, Klara, she had one close friend. And many other not-so-close friends. But two close friends can be trouble.'

Petra didn't know how to answer this. She knew that Zofia's sister had died of leukaemia when she was twelve years old. It'd happened a couple of years ago and Zofia often spoke about her. It was always awkward when she came up in conversation. Petra didn't know whether to respond or to try to ignore it in case Zofia got upset. Today she almost asked a question. 'What was Klara's best friend like?' she wanted to say and then maybe

94

compare her in some way to her best friend, Tina. But before she spoke she thought of Tina living closer to Mandy than she did. She felt a twist of anxiety in her chest and momentarily forgot about Klara.

Zofia dried her hands on the tea towel and Petra focused on her nails. Today they were yellow and had tiny pink stars stuck to them. Zofia worked in a nail shop with her friend Marya. They were always practising on each other's nails. Zofia saw her looking.

'Did I tell you Marya is going back to Poland? Her boyfriend has asked her to marry him.'

'Oh.'

'He's asked her three times before. I told her to dump him but she is in love! You can't change the mind of someone in love.'

'You'll miss her.'

'Lucky I have you. You'll be my girlfriend. And I was thinking we should go shopping. I buy you some new jeans. These are tight. I think they are old.'

Petra looked down at her jeans. They *were* old, the knees almost white and the zip fraying. She'd got taller since she'd bought them and she knew they were too short, but her trainers were bulky so it didn't really show.

'And maybe jumper?'

'Great. When?' Petra said.

'I get paid Friday. Meet me at Angel tube at five thirty and we'll go shopping.'

Zofia folded the tea towel up into a neat oblong. Then she went into the living room and Petra heard her dad speak. They were talking quietly, her dad's voice a little choppy, Zofia's

95

silky tones underneath. Petra couldn't work out if they were getting on all right or not. They'd seemed quiet while eating and her dad had been looking at his phone a lot. It was hard to understand people's relationships.

Zofia had first appeared just after Easter. She came to the flat a couple of times, then one morning she emerged from her dad's bedroom wearing his shirt and looking sleepy. Petra followed her instructions and made her a cup of tea just the way she liked it: black, two sugars, the tea bag left in for a long time. Her dad came out of the bedroom in his jeans and nothing on his top. He was smiling and Petra felt embarrassed looking at him. His skin was white and she could see the lines of his ribs. Zofia said something in Polish that Petra couldn't make out. Her dad laughed but looked at Petra and did a *Huh?* gesture with his hands.

At first Petra only saw Zofia to say hello and goodbye to. Then she went out with them a few times: to Thorpe Park, Southend and London Zoo. They would finish up at McDonald's and it was fun, but Petra always felt a little ill at ease, as if she was play-acting in some way, trying to be a *good daughter*. When Zofia asked her dad if Petra and she could go shopping together he shrugged and said, 'Fine by me.' That was when she began getting to know Zofia.

They went to lots of shopping centres: Nag's Head, Angel, Camden, Spitalfields and Walthamstow Market. Zofia liked to scavenge in charity shops but she always bought Petra something new: a top or leggings or skirt. Petra linked her arm as they strolled along, looking in the shops. They weren't really searching for anything in particular but it gave them time to chat at length. Zofia talked about her life in Poland and her family whom she didn't get on with. She also talked about her friends, the jobs she'd had, her two cats that she'd left with a friend before she came to England. She talked about her sister, Klara, who, she said, she missed every single day. While running her fingers across some china or picking up glassware Zofia unspun her life story for Petra.

When Petra got home from these outings she would tell her dad something. 'Did you know that Zofia went to a school where the only teachers were nuns?' And her dad would mumble some reply but she knew he wasn't really listening.

Zofia was equally interested in Petra's life. Petra told her everything there was to know about Tina and also about the years when her gran had been alive. Then it was the summer holidays and she was getting ready to go to secondary school. Tina was away with her mum a lot so Petra had of time to kill. She spent time at the nail shop tidying up the equipment and sweeping the floor. In return she had her nails done for free several times while Marya interrogated her about her dad and then said things in Polish to Zofia.

She'd stayed at Zofia's house a few times, sleeping in her bed while Zofia slept on a fold-out bed alongside. She'd met different people, mostly from Poland, who came and stayed in the house-share with Zofia and then moved on. Zofia was the only one who was there long term. She'd been to Marya's flat and seen her boyfriend who was also from Poland and worked on a building site. Sometimes, when she was at home and saw her dad getting ready to go out with *Sophie*, she quite forgot that it was the same person, as if *her* Zofia were someone different. She thought of Zofia as *her friend* and nothing much to do with her dad.

She could hear the television being switched off and moments later saw her dad come into the kitchen. The bathroom door shut then and Petra guessed that Zofia had gone to the toilet.

'I'm going to take Soph home now, Petra. You'll be OK, won't you?' he said.

'Course,' Petra said.

Her dad was looking smart again. He had some suit trousers on and a clean shirt and tie.

'I'm driving Mr Constantine tonight. The man I picked up from the airport? Just one ride then I'll be home. I couldn't turn it down because the money's so good. I won't be out all night. I'll have my mobile but you'll be all right on your own, won't you? Don't open the door to anyone.'

'I'll be all right.'

'I won't tell Soph that you'll be on your own because she worries. You're a big girl now. She doesn't get that. Don't be ringing her or anything. She fusses too much. Any problems call my mobile.'

The bathroom door opened and Petra could hear Zofia humming a tune. She came into the kitchen, walking past Petra's dad.

'You have good birthday?' Zofia said, giving her a goodbye hug.

'Come on, I haven't got all day,' her dad said, opening the front door.

Zofia said something in Polish under her breath. Then she picked up her coat from the back of the chair and gave a little wave. As she reached the front door Petra could hear her dad's voice, sharp like a pin bursting a bubble, 'Leave her alone, Soph, you're all over her, for God's sake.' Then the front door shut.

Petra sighed. It had been like this for a while now. Her dad was like a dog with a sore tooth snapping at Zofia. Zofia didn't get riled by him, she just smiled sweetly and seemed to put up with his moods. How much longer would it last? Petra wondered. She'd seen him get fed up with other girlfriends.

She tidied the kitchen and took the rubbish outside and placed it in the chute. When she closed the flat door she saw that it was seven forty. She had the whole evening to get through. She could ring Tina and see what she was doing, but she had homework that she should probably have a go at. After that she drew some designs for The Red Roses outfits and wrote out some lyric sheets of songs they could learn.

Just after ten she began to get ready for bed. Her books had been packed and she'd ironed her skirt for school the next day. In her pad she had several designs for outfits that she and Tina could wear for The Red Roses. She'd drawn the figures like matchstick girls and felt a little guilty looking at them. At the same time at least it would be clear to Mandy that she could never wear these kinds of clothes so it was a really solid reason why she could never join the group. Just in case she asked.

She lay back down on top of her duvet.

She wondered what Mandy's mother and father were like. She pictured her mother as a bit overweight and perhaps someone who didn't have a job. She probably worried all day long because Mandy was always saying, 'My mum says this, my mum wants me home early, my mum is worried about . . .' She knew that her father worked in a building society and Petra had once seen him coming out of the doctor's and waving at Mandy when they were walking home from school. Tina's mum had probably been behind the counter, saying in that polite receptionist voice of hers, 'Hello, Mr Crystal. Do you have an appointment?'

Petra thought about her own mother. She'd died when Petra was two years old. She pumped her pillow up then lay back down and chewed at the side of her lip. She had no memory of her as a person, just a pile of photographs that her gran had given her. Her name had been Megan and she'd gone up to Oxford Street to buy some clothes for a friend's wedding and got hit by a car. When Petra was ten years old her gran had taken her on the Tube and showed her the very place where it'd happened. It was an obelisk in the middle of the road near the Marks & Spencer's at Marble Arch. It was a tiny spot where pedestrians paused and waited to see if traffic was coming in the opposite direction. On that day, when her mum was shopping, it had been packed. She'd been standing on the very edge of a knot of people waiting to cross when a car had raced through the lights and lost control, hitting her with a glancing blow. *A glancing blow*. Petra had had no idea what that was at first. Her mum had been propelled across the road and had fallen on the place where the road met the pavement. Her head had hit the kerb with a crack. If she'd landed anywhere else she would have lived, her gran said.

Petra had stood beside her gran just in front of the obelisk while her gran wept loudly. Petra, who had been holding her arm, felt her whole body shivering. She held on to her tightly and avoided making eye contact with the pedestrians walking around them looking puzzled. Petra didn't cry that day, but a year later, when her gran had died, she'd sobbed until her eyes were swollen and her face was scarlet.

She heard a noise and sat up straight. It was coming from outside the front door of the flat. Was it her dad back? So early? She stepped out into the hallway and looked at the glass, lit up by the balcony lights. There was a shape and it stayed there for what seemed like a while. Then there was an exclamation, the sound of a man's voice swearing, and the bell rang.

She walked along the hall then ducked into the kitchen. There was no light on so she pulled the blind to the side. A man was standing out on the balcony. Petra had never seen him before. He was tall with long hair and was wearing a checked shirt but no coat as if he'd just jumped out of a car for a few moments. He leant close to the door and began to call out.

'Jason! Jase! You in there? I need a chat. Jason!'

Then he stopped and stepped back and leant on the balcony wall with his arms behind him. Petra wondered if he would stay there for a while, maybe wait for her dad to return. He looked like he was going to do that when he suddenly stood as if to attention, gave the front door a last knock with his fist and walked off.

She waited at the kitchen window for ages in case he came back. She thought about ringing her dad but decided not to. She wrote a note.

A man came knocking for you. He seemed quite upset. I didn't open the front door.

Then she went to bed.

Thirteen

It was Friday. It was pouring outside and they were in the dinner hall. The table they were sitting at was sticky and there was the lingering smell of food in the air. The hall was half full of students keeping out of the rain. From behind the kitchen doors came the sound of pots banging together and chatter from the dinner ladies.

'I would come but I'm going shopping with my dad's girlfriend tonight,' Petra said.

'Oh,' Tina replied.

Her face was red from where she'd been crying. Mandy had produced tissues from her bag. Petra looked at the small cellophane packet. It was brand new, unused. Mandy opened the flap and pulled a pristine tissue from inside. She shook it out and handed it to Tina who blew her nose.

'Dad wants me to stay over tonight but Mum won't let me. She says I'm not allowed to go to his flat. She doesn't want me to meet Janice.'

Tina's dad's beautician was called Janice.

'She says, as a treat, I can have someone to stay.'

'I would come over but I've promised . . .' Petra said.

It wasn't the new clothes that were uppermost in Petra's mind. She was looking forward to spending time with Zofia.

'I'll come,' Mandy said.

'Are you allowed?' Tina said, patting her nose with the tissue.

'My mum can speak to your mum on the phone and then I could come round.'

Mandy looked at Petra. Her expression was calm but her eyes appeared to sparkle.

'That's if it's all right with you, Petra.'

'Why wouldn't it be all right with me? Tina can do what she wants.'

'I know that. I just thought you might feel left out.'

The bell went for registration. Petra got up.

'Come on,' she said. 'We don't want to be late.'

She walked ahead of Tina and Mandy all the way to the classroom.

Zofia was outside Angel tube station when she got there. They edged across the busy road and went into the shopping centre. It didn't take long to buy two pairs of jeans, a jumper and a shirt. Petra was thrilled and stopped thinking about Mandy going round to Tina's house where Tina's mum would probably be making them some food and allowing them to watch whatever they liked on Tina's huge television.

They walked back to Zofia's and picked up a pizza on the way. By the time they got to her house the pizza was beginning to cool, so Zofia put it in the oven for five minutes and made Petra wash her hands and sit down at the table. She got a tub of coleslaw out and Petra grimaced. She didn't like coleslaw.

There was something unpleasant in its texture and this coleslaw had Polish writing on the outside. Zofia scooped spoonfuls of it onto her plate.

Zofia loved eating. She was always talking about food she liked and how she missed the food she had in Poland. 'Not enough meat in this country,' she said. 'No beetroot soup.' Her fridge was full of Polish products: strange-looking sausages and half-full jars of sauerkraut. It made Petra shiver to look at it.

After washing up they went into Zofia's pink bedroom. This was Petra's favourite part of her visit. The walls were painted light pink and the curtains were a deeper shade. The duvet had scarlet flowers all over it and there were scatter cushions at the top with sequins sewn on them. It was really a child's bedroom but Zofia didn't care. 'I love these colours,' she'd said. 'Why shouldn't I have pretty bedroom?'

'Can I try my stuff on?' Petra said.

'Go ahead,' Zofia said. 'Maybe I can do your nails? No school tomorrow?'

Zofia's mobile rang. She pulled it out of her jeans pocket. She mouthed, 'Marya.'

Once Petra had got one of her new pairs of jeans and the shirt on she sat on the bed and waited for Zofia to finish her phone call. She was speaking in Polish so Petra couldn't understand what she was saying but her tone was light with a few exclamations so she guessed that she and Marya were gossiping. She looked at the wall beside Zofia's bed. There were six small framed photographs. Each one of them was of her sister, Klara. Two were baby pictures but the others had been taken when she was older. Klara had short dark hair and a very serious expression. Petra peered at the picture of a small girl in what looked like a wedding dress. It was her first communion dress, Zofia had explained, because they were Catholics and it was an important ceremony for every girl. Just above Zofia's bed, attached to the wall, was a crucifix.

There were other things of her sister's too. In the past Zofia had brought out a small wooden box containing a variety of items that'd belonged to or were associated with Klara. Zofia had insisted that Petra have a look through. There was a lock of hair in a tiny plastic bag. There was a gold chain with a cross on it and two small rings. There was a passport with Klara's photo in it. When Petra opened it some photographs fell out. They showed Zofia and her sister in Paris, next to the Eiffel Tower. A couple of birthday cards were in among the things too and Petra read them, taking in the lines of kisses that started big and bold and got smaller as they marched across the page. Petra had replaced these things tidily because she knew they were important to Zofia.

'Now we are ready!' Zofia said, tossing her mobile on the bed.

Petra sat with her hand rested on the underside of a sparkly cushion. Zofia produced a bottle of deep red nail varnish.

'This one I think. For your girl band. You can take bottle and do Tina's nails. Maybe do new girl, too. So she doesn't feel left out.'

Petra frowned. Zofia raised her eyebrows.

'OK.'

'Not nice to feel left out.'

Zofia took each finger and held it in the air while she painted the nail. She was humming a tune and mouthing some words, her face tight with concentration. When she'd finished she studied the nails over.

'Is good.'

Petra started to wave her hands back and forth. Zofia looked thoughtful. Petra could tell that she was going to say something about her dad.

'Jason is a bit depressed at the moment? No?'

'He's a bit stressed,' Petra said. 'He worries about money. Being a cab driver doesn't pay a lot.'

Zofia nodded as though she'd thought as much. Then Petra noticed a dark mark at the edge of Zofia's T-shirt. Like a dirty finger mark. Zofia noticed her looking and pulled at the sleeve as if to make it longer. Petra averted her eyes, a tiny question mark flashing in her head.

'And,' Petra said, hurrying on, 'we're due a visit from the social worker in the next couple of weeks and he always gets worried when they come. They're so nosey. They want to know absolutely everything. He's afraid they might not think he can look after me. Since my gran died they come round regularly.'

'Is usual? For social worker to visit?'

'Well, no, but dad was kind of unwell after my gran died and he couldn't look after me very well so . . .'

Petra pretended that she was studying her nails. She didn't know what her dad had said to Zofia and she didn't want to contradict him.

'Your dad loves to look after you.'

There was a silence while Petra tried to think of something good to say about her dad. He couldn't handle stress, that's what her gran had said. Sometimes he was out of control of what he was doing. She didn't say this to Zofia but eyed the edge of her T-shirt and then looked her over, her eyes searching for any other marks that shouldn't be there. Zofia's forehead wrinkled up as if she knew exactly what Petra was doing. She suddenly stood up, full of energy.

'He will be here soon to pick you up! Why don't we watch some *Friends* while we wait?'

Petra nodded. Zofia loved *Friends*. Petra did too but she'd seen them all so many times that she almost knew the lines off by heart. Zofia had seen them all in Polish but it pleased her to watch them in English. She was always saying, 'This bit very hilarious,' and then laughing after it came on. Chandler Bing was her favourite. Petra's favourite had changed over the years. She'd liked each of them best at one time or another.

Her dad came about eight. The bell rang for a long time, as if he'd just kept his finger pressed on it. Zofia seemed startled and then made a dash to open the door. Petra could hear his footsteps following Zofia up the stairs. Her stuff was all packed and ready, her school clothes in her rucksack with the other new purchases.

'Hi, Dad,' she said.

His face was closed. There was no expression that she could read.

'Everything OK, Jason?' Zofia said, smiling.

The laughter from *Friends* was loud and Zofia picked up the remote and put it on mute. The room seemed bare without the noise.

'Just a fare. Didn't have the full money. I had a choice of getting the law involved or just taking what he had.'

'Never mind,' Zofia said, going on tiptoes and pulling his head downwards so that she could give him a kiss on the cheek.

'Come on then. Let's get home. Chop, chop.'

'Bye, *Kochanie*. See you soon.'

'Thanks for the clothes and the nails.'

'Thanks, Soph,' her dad said. 'I'll give you a ring.'

'Tonight? Tomorrow?'

'Maybe Sunday. I'm not sure.'

As they got into the car Petra looked back and saw Zofia standing at the garden gate. She waved to them. The car moved off and she was still waving. Petra waved back but her dad did not.

Fourteen

The music in the car was loud so there was no need to talk.
Petra looked at her dad's hands tapping on the steering wheel
in time with the beat. Now he seemed perfectly relaxed. He'd
lost the stiffness that she'd seen when he'd been at Zofia's.
From time to time he sang along with the song and when they
stopped at lights he pushed his phone at her.

'Listen to the ringtone,' he said.

She accessed the page and pressed the buttons and heard
his latest ringtone. It was a football anthem playing on a
keyboard.

'Good or what?' he said.

At least he hadn't said 'cool'.

Inside the car smelt of people. That was the problem with
having a dad who was a cab driver. Strangers left their scent
behind in his car. Sometimes they left other things: wallets,
phones, once a walking stick. Her dad said he always handed
them in to the police but Petra had found the walking stick
weeks later in his wardrobe.

They turned into Princess Street and slowed down. The
indicator was on and the car pulled up in front of number

fifty-three. Her dad turned round and pulled a plastic bag off the back seat.

'I said I'd get some ciggies for Mr Merchant,' he said. 'You OK here? I'll be five minutes.'

She nodded.

The door shut and she watched her dad walk round the front of the car and head for the house. There was one light on in the whole building. It was the living room, although her dad had described it as a kind of bedsit room. The street lamp threw light onto the front garden. It looked stuffed full with shady clumps of hedge and other bushes spreading across it.

Her dad had unhooked the front gate and walked around the front garden, heading for a side door to the back garden. He seemed to have a bit of trouble opening it but then he went through and closed it behind him.

She wondered if Mr Merchant had heard the sound of the gate and knew that someone was coming to see him. Petra knew cigarettes were not a good thing to bring for somebody in ill health but her dad had told her that Mr Merchant was old and lonely and that a few ciggies weren't going to make things any worse for him. Mr Merchant had a carer who came in to see him once every day but she was not allowed to bring him anything like that. Her dad had known Mr Merchant for a while. When he wasn't so ill he'd used his cab frequently but in the last year he hardly went out. He even had to use ambulances for hospital out-patient appointments.

Her dad said it was his way of doing a good deed.

It made her feel *proud* for a moment. Mr Merchant was old and lonely. Most people in the road probably didn't know he existed but her dad made an effort, even if it was just for cigarettes. She watched him emerge from the gate at the side of the house. His coat was flaring out behind him. He was smiling. She wished he'd been smiling when he'd called at Zofia's for her.

'That's done,' he said.

'Is he well enough to let people in?' Petra said.

'No. Poor old bloke sits in a chair or stays in bed. There's a key on a hook by the back door. It's hidden by ivy so only people he trusts know about it.'

Petra smiled at her dad. Mr Merchant *trusted* him.

'Off we go,' he said.

When they got home there was a man outside the door of the flat. He was leaning back against the balcony as though he hadn't expected anyone to be in. Petra recognised him at once. It was the man who had come to the door a few evenings before. Tonight he looked rough. His hair was sticking up and his lip was swollen as if someone had punched it.

'All right, Jason?' the man said as they got closer.

'All right, Nathan,' her dad said, his voice offhand as though he wasn't particularly pleased to see him.

Petra gave a polite smile and used her key to open the front door.

'Go on in, Petra. Shut the door. I'll be in in a minute,' her dad said.

Petra closed the door behind her. The flat was cold so she turned the central heating on. She went into her room and tipped out her rucksack. She sorted the contents into three piles: her new clothes, her uniform and her school books. Then she went into the living room, picked up the remote and put the television on. She flicked around for a few moments to see what was on. She left it on and walked into the hallway. Her dad was still talking to the man. The conversation outside was loud and they were interrupting each other. She wondered if they were having a row or just an animated conversation. She headed for the kitchen but paused when she heard a familiar name.

'Merchant.'

She stood very still and listened.

'Don't feel sorry for him, Jason. If he can't pay then he'll have to suffer the consequences. It's not personal. It's business. That's all.'

'Leave it. I'll sort it out. Don't get involved. Leave him to me.'

'As long as you're OK with it.'

The sound of her dad's key in the door made her dart into the kitchen and straight across to the fridge. She opened it and stared inside as her dad came into the room.

'Petra? You OK?'

'Yes,' she said, taking out a can of drink and closing the door.

'That was an old mate of mine.'

'He was the man who came round the other night,' she said, taking a gulp of fizzy drink.

'Nathan Ball. He was the one who helped me get the driving job.'

She wanted to say something. *Why were you talking about Mr Merchant?* Instead she just fiddled with the cold can that was in her hand. Her dad's eyes dropped to her hands. His face creased up.

'What is that rubbish on your nails? Did Soph do that?'

Petra nodded, confused. Zofia had done her nails lots of times. He had never said anything about them before. He swore under his breath and his mouth hardened.

'I don't like it, Petra. You're . . . That colour makes you look . . . Well, like a *tart* . . .'

'It's just for the girl band,' she said.

'You're only twelve. I don't want you going out looking like that. She's got no right to . . .'

'It wasn't her idea.'

'I told her to lay off. She just goes ahead and does what she wants . . . She takes no notice of what I say!'

'No, I *asked* her to. I think *I* picked the colour.'

Her dad's face had flattened out. Things were going through his head, Petra knew, but she had no idea what he was thinking. He walked a few paces then turned and leant on the worktop. She could only see his back, his shoulder squared off like he was a door closed against her. The atmosphere was uncertain. She tensed herself, her eyes screwed up, ready for something.

'I'll take it off, Dad. I've got nail varnish remover. But like I said don't blame Zofia. I asked her to.'

He seemed to deflate. He turned back and exhaled loudly. She'd misread him. He was just momentarily angry. There would be no trouble tonight.

'I'll get rid of it now,' she said, walking past him.

He caught her arm though and held it. His hand was like a loose cuff on her elbow. She braced herself in case he tightened his grip.

'Don't get too close to Soph. She could just pack up and go back to Poland at any time. She's a nice girl but . . .'

He let her arm go. She went to her bedroom and closed the door behind her. He hadn't hurt her but she still felt emotional, as if she might cry. She heard the volume of the television go up and she walked towards her drawers, searching for the nail varnish remover and cotton wool pads. She sat on her bed and began to wipe the colour off her nails. The cotton wool became quickly red, as if it were mopping up blood from a wound. She used one after the other and placed them on her bedside cabinet in a line. The smell of the liquid was strong and medicinal.

Her dad was wrong.

Zofia wouldn't go back to Poland. She liked it here.

Fifteen

On the way home from school Petra bought some things from the supermarket. When she got back to the flat it felt boiling hot, as if the heating had been on all day. She walked through to the living room and found her dad lying on the sofa. His eyes were closed and he looked unconscious. She could see that he was drunk. On the carpet beside him was a line of seven empty beer cans. She went into the kitchen and saw, with dismay, a bottle of vodka that was half full.

He'd probably been drinking all afternoon.

She leant against the fridge, disheartened. Things had been better for the last week and a half. Ever since the night he'd got upset about her wearing the nail varnish he seemed to have made an effort. He'd been up early every morning getting off to work and looking smart, being cheerful. He'd done a few extra jobs for Mr Constantine and he'd bought some new clothes. He'd been out with Zofia a few times and seemed happy when Petra spoke about her.

Now he was drunk again. And the social worker was due to visit the next day.

Wearily, she went back into the living room, picked up the

cans and began to tidy up, sidestepping her dad and the sofa. She opened the window and straightened the footstool and the coffee table. In the kitchen she tightened the lid on the vodka bottle and put it into the cupboard. Then she put her bag in her bedroom and went into the bathroom. There, on the glass shelf above the sink, was a make-up bag. It was neon pink with black squiggles on it. It belonged to Zofia and inside was a mascara wand and a lipstick, the only make-up she wore. She had obviously been in the flat earlier. She must have left it behind. Possibly she had left *before* her dad had got drunk.

Petra made herself a grilled cheese sandwich which she ate in her bedroom. She got changed and sorted out her school clothes for the next day. Then, just before six, she left the flat to go to Tina's and rehearse The Red Roses. They'd made the arrangement earlier at school while Mandy had been doing something else. Petra was glad to have somewhere to go. Maybe, when she got home, her dad would have stumbled off into bed.

At Tina's they rehearsed The Red Roses in her bedroom. They dressed up in their outfits: black leggings, oversized red T-shirts and hair held back with bands with red silk roses on them. There had been a debate about shoes: high heels or pumps? Petra had decided on black pumps because it made it easier to move around.

They were in front of a long mirror in Tina's bedroom.

'Ta dah!' Tina said.

'Stand back to back,' Petra said.

Tina turned and they stood sandwiched together. Petra could see their reflection. They were the same height. She smiled at this. It was a good look; as if they were two sides of a mirror image.

'Side by side,' Petra said.

Tina's hair was big. They'd have to use straighteners. The rest was fine though. They were the same height, the same weight. They both had pale skin and dark hair. They looked like sisters. Or twins. Petra liked that idea. If Tina had been her sister she would have been very happy. Petra counted, 'One . . . two . . . three . . .' and they began to sing.

Ever since primary school Tina had been a fixture of Petra's life. They'd sat together in year four and found that they'd both read the same books and comics and liked the same games. When they were first friends they'd played a make-believe game that lasted for weeks. 'Imagine there'd been a plane crash,' Petra said, 'and almost everyone drowned. You and me managed to swim to the shore of an island.' There was a lot to do in this game: draw the island, name it, build shelter, find food, deal with hostile animals and other shipwrecked people. They had to nurse each other through injuries using imaginary bandages and crutches. They had to write letters and put them in bottles and launch them into the sea. The local park had a pond which had a small island in the middle. No one was allowed on it but the sight of it fuelled their game and they played on, day after day. There was hope of rescue but it never came because then the game would end. It gave Petra an amazing world to think about: her and Tina living together twenty-four hours a day, Tina's parents and her dad *all gone*. No school, no one telling them what to do, just two kids surviving, helping themselves. It made Petra feel strong, in charge of herself and the things that happened to her. Tina was happy to play. Tina was happy with Petra. Petra *loved* Tina.

As they grew older there were other games but in time these lessened their hold and the talk changed to computer games, magazines, bands and clothes. Tina had been around a lot when Petra's gran died and had helped her with the move from her gran's house to the flat. When they went to secondary school they had to grow up quickly. There was no make-believe there, just getting from place to place, turning up at the right classrooms, not looking stupid. The best thing to do, Petra decided, was to look at what the older kids were doing and emulate them. See how they carried themselves round the building, where they sat, how they behaved. Petra and Tina could copy them, become mature, divide themselves off from the year sevens who were still tearing around the playground yearning for their old primary school classrooms and teachers.

This was how The Red Roses were born.

Petra and Tina practised their best song over and over. At the end of an hour or so they both collapsed on Tina's bed, breathless and laughing.

'I'll be in school late tomorrow,' Petra said.

'How come?'

'Social worker visit.'

'Shall I save you a seat in history?'

'No. I don't know how long it'll take. I'll text you when I'm on my way.'

'How's your thumb?' Tina asked.

Petra frowned as she looked down at the top of her thumb. The red line of the cut was still there.

'I think it'll leave a scar,' Tina said dramatically.

She offered her thumb to Petra who placed her own on top of it.

'You didn't tell Mandy?'

Tina shook her head. Petra believed her.

It was just gone eight when Petra left Tina's. She slipped out of the front door without saying goodbye to Tina's mum because she knew that she'd be anxious about her walking home in the dark on her own. She would offer to walk with her or give her a lift and Petra would say, 'But it's only a few streets away,' and Tina's mum would *tsk* and fuss.

She walked along Princess Street and paused when she got alongside fifty-three. She hadn't looked at the house for a while. Mandy's presence on the walk home from school had kept her away from it. She stopped and leant on the wall. The light was on in the downstairs room but the rest was pitch-black. Her eyes settled on the upstairs rooms. Mr Merchant had lived in this house for many years, her dad had told her. He'd had a wife but they'd got divorced years ago. He also had two sons but they both lived abroad. Tina's mum knew bits about him because she worked in the doctor's surgery he used. Once the house must have been full of light as Mr Merchant's family busied themselves in every room. Even the back garden would have been lit up by the light from boys' bedrooms.

Now it was like a dark ship, with a single light on the bridge.

A car shot past behind her, music coming from inside. She turned and saw it turn the corner out of the street. Across the road, at the newsagent's, a few kids from school were hanging around. One of them called out to her but she didn't answer.

She looked back to the old house. There were roses poking above the wall that she hadn't noticed before. The curtain moved at the window of the room that was lit up. Light spilt into the garden. Petra peered through the bushes. She went on her tiptoes to get a better view. The curtain moved further back and she saw a person there staring out.

Was it Mr Merchant?

It was the face of an old man. He might have had glasses on, she thought, but she couldn't be sure. One of his hands was stretched up, holding the curtain back. She moved along the wall until she was under the street lamp. Now she had an unrestricted view. Mr Merchant was wearing a shirt and tie. She frowned at this. A disabled old man wearing formal clothes? In her head she'd pictured him as very frail, wearing a chunky cardigan. She'd certainly imagined him in an armchair or a wheelchair and possibly with a plastic tube in his nose and an oxygen tank within arm's reach. She hadn't thought, from what her dad had said, that he would have the strength to stand up and go over to the window or that he would be wearing normal clothes.

She stared at him. And she found herself doing an odd thing.

She lifted her hand and waved at him. She did it two or three times, not sure if he would see her at all. But he was gazing in her direction and after a moment he raised his other arm and waved back at her.

Then the curtain dropped and he was gone.

Huh! she thought. She'd *seen* Mr Merchant, the recluse.

She remembered the cigarettes her dad had bought for him. It was a charitable act of sorts but it gave her an uneasy feeling. *Something* wasn't quite right but she wasn't sure what it was. She began to walk in the direction of home. She went slowly, taking tiny steps and stopping at shop fronts to look in, even though there was nothing of interest to her inside. Nathan Ball came into her mind. She pictured him on the balcony outside their front door. She didn't like him, she decided. She didn't like what he'd said: *He'll have to pay the consequences* . . . and the way he'd said *Merchant*. Not *Mr* Merchant, which was only polite when talking about an old, ill pensioner.

When she got to the flats she rummaged in her bag for her key. Her fingers hit something soft, unusual. She pulled it out and smiled. It was Zofia's make-up bag.

Tomorrow she would go to the nail bar and give it back to her.

Sixteen

Pam Fellows, the social worker, was due at ten.

Her dad was tidying up while Petra had her breakfast. She was standing up in the kitchen eating toast and listening to him humming a song in-between bouts of vacuuming in the living room. He didn't appear to have any kind of hangover. He was cheerful. He'd brought a cup of tea into her bedroom as he woke her up and left her a five pound note next to it.

'Sorry about yesterday. I was a bit stressed and had a bit too much to drink,' he'd said, making a *click-click* noise with his tongue. He wasn't the same man that she'd seen almost comatose on the sofa the previous evening.

Pam Fellows arrived at ten past ten. Petra's dad let her in and Petra could hear her apologising for being late and her dad downplaying it as they came into the living room. He gestured towards the sofa for her to sit down, saying he was just going to put the kettle on.

Pam was wearing a beige trouser suit. Round her neck she had an identity tag and hanging alongside it a pen. She was carrying a striped bag with shoulder straps which looked big enough to hold a change of clothes. Petra had seen it before and knew it held her laptop and files and an assortment of different little notepads. 'I can't resist buying stationery,' she'd said in the past.

'Hi, Petra. How are you? You're looking well.'

Petra nodded. She was wearing her school uniform. She wondered if she should say something about the way Pam looked. Pam had a very round face. She had a round body too, her middle straining over the top of her trousers. She wore lots of jewellery: beads round her neck, earrings, bracelets, rings. 'I can't walk past anything that glitters,' Pam had said. 'I'm always buying earrings.'

'I like your necklace,' Petra said.

Pam picked it up and smiled down at it. 'This was a present from my sister.'

The door opened.

'I can't remember, Pam. Sugar? Milk?' her dad said.

'One sugar, a dash of milk, thank you, Jason.'

Then she rifled about in her bag and pulled out a file.

'Right,' she said, sorting through some papers, 'it's been ages since I saw you. Must be three months or more. Certainly before you went to Cromarty High. How are you settling into school?'

'It's OK. I like it there. I'm getting high grades.'

'That's good news.'

Her dad appeared with a tray on which sat three mugs and a plate of biscuits.

'Here we are,' he said.

While they drank their tea Pam talked to her dad about his job and the flat. Then she spoke to him about his health and his counselling sessions. Petra sipped her drink. She held her knees tight together and her elbows close to her ribs. She smiled every now and then to show that she wasn't tense. She looked at Pam's shoes sticking out from under her trousers. They had pointed toes and high heels. No doubt when she took them off her trouser bottoms dragged along the carpet.

'Don't you think so, Petra?'

She nodded, not sure of what her dad had said.

He was looking smart. He'd shaved that morning and was wearing a shirt underneath a V-neck jumper. He had chinos on and he'd polished his shoes.

'. . . that we'd love a house and garden. Somewhere to grow our own vegetables. But we're low down on the housing list.'

To grow our own vegetables. Had her dad really said that? It sounded like something that Zofia might say. It sounded like the very thing Zofia might do. She pictured her in jeans and wellies (with heels), walking across a garden with a handful of carrots that she'd just pulled out of the ground. Her dad was talking on about Petra's good work at school and how her teachers had said she was very promising.

Pam put her hand into her stripy bag and picked out a small spiral-bound notebook. On the front of it was a diamanté butterfly.

'I think it would be good if I could have some time on my own with Petra?' Pam said.

'Of course,' her dad said, standing up and patting his pockets. 'I've got a number of jobs to do this morning. So, Petra, I'll see you about quarter to six? Will you put the shepherd's pie in the oven?'

124

Petra nodded. Her dad picked up some papers from the coffee table.

'I'll see you soon, Pam. Remember what I said: give me a bell if you ever want to talk.'

'I will. Thank you, Jason.'

He went out and Pam smiled while she waited for the front door to close.

'Right. There are just a couple of things I want to ask you about. First one is your attendance. How's it been at Cromarty?'

'I've just missed a couple of days,' Petra said. 'That's all.'

'You've only been there a month.'

'I had a bad headache.'

'For two days?' Pam said, screwing her face up.

'I felt ill,' Petra said.

'Did you go to the doctor's?'

'I took some pills.'

'So you didn't go to the doctor's?'

Petra shook her head.

'We've talked about this, Petra. One day off can lead to another and another and this year you were going to try to have one hundred per cent attendance.'

'I know I won't take any more time off.'

Pam made notes in the diamanté book. She looked at her watch. Then she turned a clean page.

'And have there been any issues with your father?'

Petra shook her head.

'Has he continued to have problems with alcohol?'

'No,' she said. 'He still drinks a bit but not like he did last year . . .'

125

She managed to keep eye contact with Pam. She didn't want to sound anything other than completely honest about this. Her dad's lifestyle worried the social workers and she didn't want to hear them talking about foster placements again.

'Because,' Petra carried on, looking straight at the social worker, 'he drives a cab so he's not allowed to drink the night before he drives. He only has some beers at the weekend.'

'And has he been able to control his temper?'

'Yes, most definitely,' she said firmly, even though it seemed like her tongue was quivering.

'And you've not felt threatened in any way?'

'No,' Petra said.

'It's very important that things don't slide back to the way they were.'

'They're not sliding back.'

'You've got my numbers on your mobile? You know you can call me during the day or you can contact the twenty-four-hour helpline. If you're worried at all . . .'

'I'm not. We're fine. We're happy. You don't need to come and see us any more. My dad's got a really nice girlfriend and if he gets married again I'll have a stepmother. Maybe we'll get a house with a garden like Dad said.'

Pam stared at her for a few seconds. Petra wondered if there was a battle going on inside the social worker's head. Could she believe Petra? Could she be sure that Petra's dad wasn't going to get blind drunk and injure her again?

Pam exhaled and seemed to come to a conclusion. She looked away and put her book and her pen into her bag. She hadn't used the pen round her neck. Petra wondered if she ever used it or if it'd just been something she had to buy. 'I can't resist buying unusual pens,' she might have said if Petra had mentioned it.

'So I'll be in touch and I'll see you before Christmas.'

'OK.'

'You're off to school now?'

'Yes.'

'Take care, my dear. Let me know immediately if anything bothers you. Promise me?'

'I will.'

'Meanwhile I'll speak to your head of year at Cromarty and check that all is well there.'

Something occurred to Petra.

'The teachers at school, do they know about what happened last year?'

'The head of year does. He has to know, Petra. He has to be on the lookout for any signs . . .'

Bruises.

Petra held her elbows tight to her chest. The unspoken word sounded between them.

'We cannot have you hurt, Petra.'

She'd only seen the head of year at assemblies. She was sure he didn't know who she was. She hoped he hadn't said anything to anyone. She didn't like to think about teachers in the staffroom talking about her dad.

'It just happened once. Never again. Dad was very low. Nan had just died. He . . .'

'I understand what you're saying, but in order for us to allow your dad to look after you we have to be sure he's dealing with those problems he had then.'

'He is. He's seeing the counsellor.'

'Good! Let's leave it there.'

Petra showed Pam to the front door. Pam talked on for a bit and Petra nodded and smiled. Eventually she left and Petra felt herself slump against the wall with relief. She went into the living room and put the mugs back onto the tray by the side of the uneaten biscuits. She carried them into the kitchen and returned the biscuits to the tin and put the mugs in the sink with some water in them.

Then she grabbed her schoolbag and left.

She didn't go straight to school. She headed for the nail shop where Zofia worked. She knew this wasn't the right thing to do. If Pam knew she would be put out, but Pam's visits always made Petra feel like doing a ten kilometre walk. There were things Petra had to get out of her system, stuff that had been talked about that she had to put back in place. Like what happened last summer. That was something she didn't want to think about.

Petra turned onto Holloway Road and walked purposefully along. Her hand was in her bag, touching the soft make-up case that Zofia had left behind. She wondered if Zofia might suggest they go shopping again, then she could go back to her pink bedroom and curl up beside her on the bed and watch *Friends* over and over.

She stopped outside the shop and looked through the window. She couldn't see Zofia, just the man in charge who Zofia called the 'Big Boss'. He was talking to a young girl standing by the reception counter. She had a bag hanging over her shoulder that was covered in fringes. Further inside the shop were a couple of other women sitting at small tables opposite customers.

She walked into the shop.

Just then a door behind the Big Boss opened and Zofia came out backwards. She was carrying some boxes and she turned to place them on the counter. Petra was just about to say hello to her when she saw Zofia's face. One of her eyes was bruised. It was a deep purple colour. The white of her eye was blood red. She'd been hit.

Petra was shocked and yet at the very same moment she wasn't a bit surprised. Not a bit. Zofia looked shamefaced, as if *she'd* done something wrong. She put one hand over her injured eye.

'What happened?'

Even as Petra asked she knew the answer. She pictured her dad lying drunk on the sofa the previous day, surrounded by empty beer cans. There'd been other girlfriends, years before when they'd lived with her gran. One of them had come to the house with a split lip and swollen jaw. Her sister had been in a small red car waiting for her. Gran had said her dad wasn't in but the girl had screamed down the hall about going to the police. When her dad appeared he'd swivelled his finger at the side of his head, implying that the girl was a bit mad.

Zofia took her hand away from her eye and forced a short laugh.

'I tripped and knocked into cupboard. I was a little drunk. Serve me right.'

The Big Boss was looking at them. The girl with the fringy bag was staring at Zofia's eye.

'I tripped,' Zofia repeated.

The Big Boss made an audible huffing sound.

'I brought your make-up bag,' Petra said, holding out the neon-pink bag.

Zofia took it. She smiled at Petra. The bruised eye crinkled up at the side.

'I like that bag,' Petra said, looking away from her face.

'I get you one,' Zofia said.

'I have to get back to school.'

Petra left the shop but paused at the glass window and waved. Zofia was still holding the make-up bag as she blew a kiss at her.

Seventeen

It was a teacher-training day and there was no school. Petra and Tina and Mandy had just had lunch at Tina's house. That morning they'd been to the shopping mall at Angel and Tina had bought some jeans and Mandy a jumper. Petra had spent money on some patterned tights. They'd all shopped for small things that were on sale: key rings, hair ties, sunglasses, make-up bags and pairs of earrings. They'd spent all their money. Petra's dad had given her some cash and now it was all gone. He'd been generous since the social worker visit. He'd also been cheerful and chatty. Things were still stilted between them though. She knew that he thought it was because he'd been drunk. He had no idea that she'd seen Zofia's black eye.

Zofia had not been mentioned at all.

The three girls walked towards the newsagent's shop. It was a bright autumn day and Petra was warm and had tied her sweatshirt round her waist. The sun was shining and Tina and Mandy were wearing the sunglasses they'd bought. Petra's were in her bag back at Tina's. She didn't mind because she was concentrating on her phone. She'd sent several texts to Zofia since the previous week. An hour before, when they were starting lunch, she'd sent another. She'd not yet had any replies.

'I say we have a look at some magazines and get ideas for making collages for posters,' Mandy said.

'Posters for what?' Petra said, poking her phone into her pocket, making sure that the top was sticking out in case she got a beep for a message.

'The Red Roses. We could make posters, like they have in Tube stations. You know the fly posters for different groups and bands?'

'Yes,' Tina said, 'Mandy and me went to look at them the other day. They're good.'

'But why? Where would we put them?'

'Well, we'd just make them and keep them. I'd like one up in my bedroom.'

'You're not even part of the group,' Petra said.

'She is, in an *advisory* way,' Tina said tentatively, 'because I've been thinking that she could be a kind of manager or coach or something.'

Petra was exasperated. Mandy had wormed her way in and now she was close to becoming something in The Red Roses. She was like an unstoppable force. Right from the start Mandy had *known* it was just Petra and Tina and she'd been happy with that. Then she began *asking* about the group, *discussing* stuff about the songs and the dances and *commenting* on their performances. Now she was talking about promotion, making posters. She was making herself indispensable.

'Her opinions are really good,' Tina said, looking hopefully at Petra.

Petra shrugged. What did she care? She had more important things to worry about: her dad and Zofia for one. Were they still a couple? She fingered her phone in her pocket and just stopped herself taking it out and looking at the screen for some message which might have slipped through the ether without making a sound.

'What we could do,' Mandy said, eying Petra, as if for permission, 'is browse the magazines, then collect some old copies – my mum says there are loads left in the doctor's surgery – and then we could make the collages on a sleepover at my house on Saturday night!'

'Did your mum say that was OK?' Tina said.

'She'll be fine about it. We can all use sleeping bags in the living room.'

'I haven't got a sleeping bag,' Petra said.

'We've got spare. It'll be fun. We can watch a movie.'

Tina was smiling, almost jumping up and down. *Why not?* Petra thought. Just then a beep came from her pocket and startled her. She turned and walked a few paces from the others to look at the message. It was from Zofia. She accessed it.

**I have make-up bag for you. Come to lunch
on Sunday if your dad allows. 1pm xxx**

She sent an answer straight away.

**I will. Dad's working on Sunday.
See u at 1 ☺**

She put her phone away and found herself smiling. Tina and Mandy were standing close together, talking about the sleepover. Mandy's shoulder was touching Tina's and she was saying something that was making Tina laugh. They looked like a pair, both of them wearing sunglasses. It gave her a sore feeling in her throat. Maybe the two of them should be The Red Roses and she should be the one on the outside. She walked slowly back over to them. Did it matter that Mandy was a fixture? She had to control her feelings. A night spent at her house would be good. She could stay there and go straight to Zofia's for lunch. Her dad would be out anyway.

'I think the posters are a good idea,' she said grudgingly.

'OK. Let's go and look at the magazines,' Mandy said.

'You go. I'll wait for you,' she said.

They went into the shop. Petra glanced around the street. Her eyes settled on Mr Merchant's dilapidated house. The building looked quite pretty from this distance; its brickwork and the foliage of the front garden gave it a country appearance. She wondered if the back garden was as overgrown as the front.

Then, just as she was about to turn away, a car pulled into the street and stopped along from number fifty-three. It was her dad's cab. Surprised, she watched as the door opened and he got out of the driver's seat. Then he opened the back door and leant in, pulling out two carrier bags of shopping. He closed it with his foot and walked towards the old house. Moments later he went through the side gate.

Her dad was like two different people. Today he was doing a kindness for an old man and yet a few days ago he'd hit out at Zofia, just as he'd done with previous girlfriends. Just as he'd done with Petra. She peeked in at the newsagent's. The others were *still* looking at magazines so she walked along the street and across the road to her dad's cab. She stood by the front of it and moments later he came back out of the side gate and through the front garden.

'Hi,' she said.

He looked taken aback.

'I thought you were at Tina's?'

'I am. We just came to the shop. Were you visiting Mr Merchant?'

'Just a bit of shopping. I didn't stop because he's fast asleep. They give him lots of drugs for the pain.'

Petra pictured the key that her dad had told her about hanging on a hook by the back door. It was covered up with ivy, he'd said.

'I'll tell you what though,' her dad said, patting her on the arm, 'that garden's like a jungle. The whole place needs clearing out. Are you OK?'

'Sure,' she said woodenly.

'I'll be a bit late. Tea about seven? How about chicken and chips? Those nice crinkle-cut ones?'

'If you like . . .'

He drove off just as she heard her name being called from behind. She looked across the road and saw Tina and Mandy outside the shop. They'd taken their sunglasses off. They were both laughing at something and the sight of it irritated Petra.

'What's up?' she said.

'Mr Johnson fancies Tina!'

Mr Johnson was the newsagent.

'No, he doesn't,' Tina said.

'He offered her a free magazine and he always comes up close to her. I think he's in love with you!' Mandy said gleefully.

'Don't be ridiculous,' Petra said, looking at them both with disdain.

Mandy's face closed up. Tina pulled at the sleeves of her top. They hung over her hands. Petra made a sudden decision.

'Let's go into the garden of the old house. We can slip round the side,' she said in a loud whisper.

They both looked baffled.

'The *house*. Let's go in now. Just to the garden! In and out.'

'Why?' Mandy said.

Petra ignored the question and focused on Tina. She stared straight at her, pushing Mandy out of her eyeline.

'You remember, Tina. We said we'd go inside once but we never did. We can slip into the garden and back out again without anyone knowing. You don't have to come if you don't want to, Mandy.'

'I didn't say I wasn't coming!'

'Come on, then. Just follow me to the side door. We stay five minutes. Have a look around then come out. It'll be a dry run for going *inside* the house.'

That was something she'd wanted to do once. She'd told Mandy about the house ever since she'd wormed her way into their friendship. She'd wanted to see the cobwebby rooms and hear the ghostly sounds from upstairs. Somehow those plans had got pushed away over the last weeks.

'Don't let's think about it. Let's do it as a dare. I dare us to go into the garden . . .'

'You can't dare yourself!' Mandy said.

'I dare you two to go in. Now, Tina, you dare me.'

'I dare you to go into the garden, Petra.'

'Now we've got to go.'

Petra strode off across the street, not at all sure whether Tina would follow her and not caring whether Mandy came as well. When she got to the front gate she saw the two of them a little behind. Mandy was there but she could tell, by her body language, that she didn't want to be.

'We can do the magazines, later,' Petra said in a loud whisper, hoping that her words showed how *fair* she could be.

Mandy stepped forward.

'When we go in the front gate we turn right immediately and cut across the front of the garden then down the side. There's a gate there.'

'How do you know?' Tina said.

'My dad is Mr Merchant's friend. He told me.'

'You'd better not get caught then!' Mandy said.

'We won't get caught. He sleeps a lot, my dad said. Follow me.'

Petra looked up and down the street. There was no one around. She led them through the front garden to the side gate. She pulled it towards her as she had seen her dad do. She held it open while the other two went in. Then she followed. It was a like a jungle, her dad had been right about that. There were green tendrils reaching out from every direction. Underfoot the path was overgrown and the wall to her side was matted with a creeping plant. Ahead of her Tina and Mandy were

137

walking side by side and then Mandy strode ahead, as though it were her excursion and not Petra's. That was the thing about Mandy. She would take over things if she could.

'Hang on!' Petra said in a loud whisper.

But Mandy was trudging through the garden as if she were some kind of explorer. Tina seemed torn. She looked round at Petra and then back at Mandy. Petra shrugged and Tina followed after Mandy. The garden was huge. There were sheds at the back which sat in the shade of a couple of giant trees. Their branches reached out across the garden and on one of them was an old swing. The ropes were there although the seat looked as if the edges of it had been eaten away by something. A light breeze ruffled the foliage and the branches swayed a little but the swing didn't seem to move; it just hung completely still as if it hadn't swung for years.

Petra turned to look at the back of the house. The upstairs windows had curtains drawn across them but the downstairs ones did not. They were thick with grime but she still looked at them cautiously, half expecting to see the old man's face again, his hand up waving at her. She could hear Tina talking loudly from behind her and wanted to shush her but her eye was drawn to the door through which her dad went in and out of Mr Merchant's home. It was surrounded with close-knit ivy which had come from a trellis further along. It had travelled across the brickwork as if it were intent on gaining entry to the house. Her eye searched through the thick strands until she saw the glint of a key hanging from a hook. She picked it off. It was a Chubb-type key and attached to it was a leather key ring. It had some initials on it: 'GM' in italics. Were they Mr Merchant's initials?

A voice sounded. It made her jump.

She spun round to loud shouts. Tina and Mandy were running back down the garden, heading for the side passageway. She looked towards the house next door and saw a man standing by a broken fence. He was wearing black glasses and his face was red, his words booming angrily across the bushes and overgrown grass. 'What on earth do you think you are doing?' He was big, his belly hanging over his trousers, a split at the bottom of his shirt where the buttons wouldn't fasten. She turned, lowered her head and walked swiftly to the corner and then ran out of the garden hurriedly, closing the gate behind her. The others had gone and as she stepped onto the pavement she saw their backs disappearing round the corner.

She followed them, running as fast as she could. When she turned out of Princess Street she saw they had stopped about twenty metres on. Tina was standing puffing, one hand on a wall. Mandy was beside her with a frightened look on her face. She walked up to them.

They all stared at each other.

They'd been chased out of the garden by the next-door neighbour.

'Do you think he'll tell my mum?' Mandy said.

Moments before she'd been the intrepid explorer and now she was falling apart. Petra shook her head. Tina started to laugh and it made Petra smile.

'Did you see his face? Like a strawberry!'

'And his belly,' Petra said, sticking her stomach out as if she were pregnant. She put on a deep voice. 'What on earth do you think you are doing?'

'Don't worry, Mandy. He doesn't know who we are,' Tina said.

Mandy seemed to relax. She dropped her hands and her mouth loosened, and she gave a weak smile. Moments later they walked back towards Tina's. They took a long circuitous route so that they didn't have to go along Princess Street again.

Petra thought about the garden though, and the Chubb key, and she wondered why her dad had bought shopping for Mr Merchant when he had carers to do that sort of thing for him.

Eighteen

Zofia was wearing a red dress. On top of that was a floral apron. There was no bruise around her eye and she had mascara on again. She looked like the old Zofia.

'Come in! Lunch almost ready.'

The house was warm and there was a strong smell of cooking. Petra slipped her coat off immediately and hung it on the hall stand. In the hallway were two suitcases. Maybe there were some new people in the house. She went into the kitchen. Zofia was on her own. There was steam, rising from a pot on the stove. Zofia's back was to her and she was humming. Petra went to say something but didn't. The kitchen table was set with two places. At each place was a stemmed glass. Zofia collected them in charity shops. She liked the ones with floral patterns best. She had a shelf full of them. The room looked welcoming but there was something not quite right – Petra could feel it, like a vague smell that she couldn't identify. There was the sound of footsteps from above. Somebody was in; Petra didn't know who it was because the people staying in the house were always changing.

Zofia turned to her. She beamed a smile.

'Sunday roast. Chicken and Yorkshire puddings and gravy. Is good,' she said, 'but not ready for half hour. You go and watch television in my room – *Friends* DVD there. I will come up in a minute.'

'OK.'

Petra headed upstairs for Zofia's bedroom. When she got there she saw that things had been moved round. There were some clothes folded in a pile and the ironing board was leaning against the wall. There was a clothes horse by the radiator where Zofia had hung some of her blouses to dry and she could see the legs of tights hanging down. The *Friends* DVD was placed on the bed.

The room felt different. She looked around. There was something missing or it just seemed bigger today, even though it was full of drying laundry. She sat on the bed and picked up the DVD. She lay back. She didn't feel like watching it. She was tired. She'd hardly slept the previous night. It shouldn't be called a *sleepover* at all, she thought. She, Tina and Mandy had been in Mandy's living room. They'd had sleeping bags laid on top of old duvets. They'd made posters, watched films and talked and made plans for The Red Roses. Mandy's mum had allowed them in the kitchen to make snacks and take drinks whenever they wanted. Actually, the whole night hadn't been bad. They'd laughed a lot and taken hours to get to sleep. Petra smiled when she thought of it. At just gone two Mandy's mother had come down the stairs and opened the door a few centimetres. 'Lights off; time to go to sleep,' she'd whispered. They'd turned the light off and lay in the dark with only a strip of light showing below the curtains from out in the street. There had been silence for a long time and then Mandy whispered,

'Lights off; time to go to sleep,' and that set them off giggling. Then every time they were silent one of them would spurt out, 'Lights off,' until the three of them were ragged with laughter and fatigue. Somehow they had each drifted into some sort of sleep. When Petra woke up it was almost eleven. The room was grey and the others were still burrowed into the sleeping bags.

Petra sat up. There *was* something different about Zofia's room. The pictures were gone. She looked to the side of the bed and saw that most of the photographs of Klara were missing. There were just two small ones left.

The door opened and Zofia came in. She'd taken her apron off and was smiling.

'Lunch in ten minutes,' she said.

She sat on the bed beside Petra. She picked up the DVD and held it in her hand. Petra wondered whether they were just going to watch ten minutes' worth of an episode and then eat. Zofia was just fiddling with the box though, turning it right way up then sideways then flipping it over as if she were reading the information on the other side. Then she spoke.

'You know that me and your dad have broke up?'

Petra didn't answer. She didn't want to say anything. She'd been persuading herself otherwise, ever since she'd seen the black eye. She'd known it really though, in her heart, but not admitted it to herself.

'This happens,' Zofia said. 'People get along very good for a while and then they don't. Is just life.'

Petra sat very still, her elbows pushing against her ribs. She pictured Zofia's eye, the bruise dark as though it had been drawn on with charcoal.

'Did my dad hit you?' she said, her voice tiny.

'No, no. No, he didn't. The bruise you saw on this eye? No, no, I knocked into the door. I was a bit drunk. That's the truth.'

But Zofia was turning the DVD case in her fingers, quickly and deftly. Petra *felt* that she was lying. She wondered if there had been other times when he'd hit out at her. They'd been together for many months. Had there been bruises that Petra hadn't noticed, like the ones *she* tried to hide from Tina?

'So, we have lunch? And you and me are still friends. You can come and see me and we can go to Angel.'

Petra stood up.

'For a while,' Zofia said.

Zofia didn't move. There was more to come in this conversation. Petra lowered herself down onto the bed again. She took the DVD from Zofia's hands. It was series three. The one where Ross and Rachel break up. He slept with someone else because he was 'on a break', but Rachel didn't agree. It was one of Zofia's favourite episodes.

'Why *for a while*?'

'Marya is going to Poland? I told you this?'

Petra nodded.

'She has friend who is opening a hair and nail shop in Lodz. This friend has inherited money from her father and she is selling her home and . . .'

Zofia seemed to dry up and looked as though she was thinking hard.

'And to tell the story more quickly, this friend has asked Marya to work with her and build up business?'

Petra was listening hard, trying to work out where the story was going, and then she remembered the pictures that were missing from Zofia's wall.

'So, Marya said to me . . .'

'You're going back to Poland with Marya.'

'Yes.'

'Why?'

'Because it is my home. I thought here, you know, with your father . . .'

'But it might be all right. You might get back together.'

Zofia shook her head. She did it with such firmness that her ponytail moved dramatically. Her eyelids were lowered and her jaw sharp.

'No. Finished.'

'But you can't go back. You live here.'

'You can send me email. I can phone you and when I come to London again, maybe in a couple of years, we can meet up and have Pizza Express.'

Petra's mouth was dry. She didn't know what to say. She felt a dragging sense of loss even though Zofia was sitting there beside her. In her head she saw her standing holding a suitcase and a holdall. She'd be wearing her old jeans to travel in and maybe not have her nails done. She'd get on a train or plane or maybe go through the Channel Tunnel and Petra would never see her again.

'Are you going with Marya?'

'Not so soon. Marya goes in four days. We have a friend with a van and he is going to drive her things there. No, I don't go for two weeks. Our friend and the van come back for me. I go

145

thirty-first of October. Halloween. So there is plenty of time. Oh, look. I got this for you.'

Zofia opened her bedside drawer and pulled out a cosmetics bag exactly like the one that she'd left round the flat the previous week, pink with black squiggles across it.

'Now we have the same bag.'

Petra took it. Another day it would have given her a lot of pleasure; today it just seemed like a postcard from a far-off place. Zofia would be living a thousand kilometres away and Petra would only have the comfort of this gaudy little bag.

'Let us have lunch. Then we can watch some *Friends*? Yes?' Zofia said.

They sat at the kitchen table opposite each other. Petra had Coke in her stemmed glass and Zofia had some red wine. There was music coming from a radio, low and relaxing, and Zofia was talking about the Big Boss who came into the nail shop with four different girlfriends and how the staff had to pretend that each one was his *only* girlfriend. Petra wasn't really listening. She moved her food around the plate and tried to convince herself that it might still be OK, her dad might change his mind. But then something occurred to her. What if it wasn't her dad who was breaking up with Zofia? What if it was the other way round? Zofia had decided that her dad was not a good bet.

That phrase 'a good bet' came straight from her gran's mouth. 'The trouble with your dad is that he's not a good bet.' As if he were a horse in a race that he would never win. There were other things she used to say as well. 'Your dad loves you but he has trouble controlling himself. There's this line that he

146

tries to stay above . . .' Petra had pictured a line drawn with a ruler and a black felt-tip pen. 'But sometimes he slips below it, then he becomes someone else.' She'd had an image of her dad, a small figure below the line, one hand holding onto it, the rest of him dangling.

She felt herself trembling and thought that she might cry.

Zofia was still talking about the Big Boss who sent her out to buy a mobile phone for each girlfriend. 'He wanted different covers for each one. He knew his girlfriends' favourite colours!' Then she stopped speaking and there was just the sound of the radio playing. Zofia looked up from her food and stared at Petra. Her face sagged. She put down her knife and fork.

'Don't cry, *moja mała róża* . . .'

But Petra couldn't help it. Her knife and fork lay half on, half off the plate as she covered up her eyes. Tears ran down her face. She couldn't stop them. Soon Zofia would be gone and her life would seem bland, bleached of colour. She sobbed, using her fingers to flick the tears away. Zofia grabbed her hand. She held it tightly, her fingers locked around Petra's as if Petra were on the edge of a building, about to fall off.

The sound of the front door bell ringing pierced the room.

They both looked round. Petra swallowed back her tears. Zofia got up.

'Someone has forgot key. I'll be back in a minute.'

Petra pushed her plate away, most of her food uneaten. She heard Zofia open the front door. There was a brief conversation then footsteps up the hall. Zofia called out. It sounded as though she was saying, 'No, no.' The kitchen door opened part way. She heard a male voice.

'Soph, I told you. It was a one-off.'

'You need to go.'

'I never meant to lash out. How many times have I got to apologise?'

It was her dad. He came into the room and stopped speaking as soon as he saw Petra. He was astonished.

'What are you doing here?'

'I . . .'

Zofia stood in the doorway, holding the door open.

'I asked Petra for lunch. You did tell your dad?'

'I . . .'

Her dad had been working all weekend. She'd told him she had a sleepover at Mandy's house but hadn't said she was going anywhere else. Petra often didn't tell him exactly where she was going. Was she in trouble? Her dad was looking at her in a flustered way. His clothes were the same ones he'd put on the previous day. He had his car keys in his hand. His eyes looked a little puffy, as if he'd not been awake long. Had he slept in the back of his cab again?

'You have to go, Jason. I told you not to come. I don't want for Petra to see us arguing.' Zofia's voice was calm.

'Soph . . .' he said, his hands out, as if in appeal.

'Jason, Petra is *here*,' Zofia said softly.

'Petra, you go out to the car.'

'Her food is not finished, Jason.'

'Go out, Petra. We can get a McDonald's. I've got to talk to Soph.'

'There is nothing to talk about.'

'Dad, I want to stay and finish my lunch.'

148

'You go, Jason. I'll see Petra gets home OK.'

'Soph . . .'

Her dad's tone had softened. He went up close to Zofia and stroked her arm.

'Come on, Soph . . . You know me . . . You *get* me . . . I don't mean no harm . . .'

He lowered his face as if to kiss her but she pushed him back.

'Don't touch me.'

He swore and grabbed her by the tops of her arms. Petra stood up straight, her elbows clamped to her ribs. She watched as her dad walked Zofia backwards towards the sink, pushing one of the chairs out of the way with his leg. The radio was playing soft tinkly music but Zofia's face was rigid, angry, and she was speaking Polish, her words spitting out at him. Petra wasn't sure what she should do. Her dad's hands were clamped on Zofia's arms and he was shushing her as if she were a naughty child.

Zofia moved her knee upwards as if aiming at her dad's groin but she was too small and he laughed at her. Petra felt her chest puff up with indignation. She stepped forward and went towards him. With her fists she pummelled his back. She used every bit of strength she had but she could feel her blows bouncing off his jacket. He glanced round at her.

'Petra!'

'Please, stop, Dad.'

'Go out to the car!'

'Leave her alone!'

'PETRA, GO OUT TO THE CAR!'

He let go of Zofia's arms and she slumped to the side. He turned round.

'Get your coat and go out,' he said, his voice steady, low, as if with some effort he was holding his temper down.

'You go, Petra,' Zofia said, stepping round him. 'I will send you text and we can go shopping. You go now.'

Petra walked across the room and out into the hall. She picked her coat off the hall stand and went out of the front door. There was a hollow feeling in her chest, big enough for her to fall into. Her dad followed her. Behind him was Zofia. Petra stopped and looked round at her, searching for any sign of damage. There was none that she could see. Zofia had her hands on her hips and her face was blank. When she caught her eye Zofia nodded her head as if to say, *It's OK. I'm OK.* Her dad walked ahead to the car and opened it.

'Get in, Petra,' he said wearily.

'Can't I just stay here for a while?'

Her dad sighed, walked round the car and grabbed her arm.

'I'm not going to say another word, just get in the cab.'

He opened the door and pushed her into the back seat. She rubbed at the place where he'd held her. It was sore. The car screeched away from the pavement and she slid to one side of the seat, directly behind him. She didn't think he could see her. She wished she didn't have to see him.

Then she remembered the cosmetic bag. She'd left it behind.

Nineteen

Petra was tired when the bell went for the last day before half-term. There had been assessments to complete, test results to get, targets profiles to fill in. She was glad the first weeks at Cromarty High were over. By now the newness had gone and she felt that she'd been there for years. She and Tina and even Mandy had their own places. First thing in the morning they stood by the library and sheltered under the awning there if it was wet. At break they usually went to the picnic tables by the sports fields. After lunch they used the small courtyard by the sixth-form block and sat on the steps by the raggedy rock garden. She was content there; she felt as though she belonged.

After school her dad insisted that she went with him to the supermarket for a big shop. She sat in the front of the cab and stared out of the passenger window. Since the previous Sunday she'd not said much to him. She'd had her meals in her room and gone out to school and spent time with Tina. When she came face to face with him in the flat she was brief and polite, as if he were a teacher she was speaking to. He had been busy working late every day and had gone to bed almost as soon as he got home. He'd not mentioned Zofia and neither had she.

She was still hurting though. There were bruises on her arm and they would fade, but the memories wouldn't. Now Zofia would be going home to Poland.

Earlier that week Petra had sent a card. It had a picture of red roses on it. She'd kept it inside her school diary all day and finally decided on the right words to write.

> Please don't go back to Poland.
> I would miss you so much.
> Petra XXXXXX

She'd bought a stamp and posted it. It was the first thing she'd ever *posted* to anyone. She'd wondered for days whether Zofia had received it.

The supermarket was busy. At the checkouts there were queues. Petra stood a bit away from her dad and stared down at the screen of her phone as though she'd been sent dozens of texts that she had to read. She thought about the week's holiday that she had ahead of her. She was looking forward to it. Mandy had been talking about a Halloween party that her mum and dad were going to have the following weekend, saying that Petra and Tina could stay over. This had pleased Petra because the sleepover at Mandy's house had been good. It might be possible, in the long run, to get *used* to Mandy.

They packed up their shopping and put it in the back of the car. On the way home Petra decided to text Tina. She felt in her pocket for her phone but it wasn't there. Then she felt around the seat and used her feet to poke about in the foot well. She tried to think what she'd done with it.

'I think I've lost my phone,' she said, her words sounding loud in the car.

Her dad pulled over to the side of the road. They both got out and searched through the food bags. It wasn't there. Her dad was exasperated but he turned the car round and they went back to the supermarket. They looked along the cars near to where they'd parked. Petra retraced her route from there to the checkout. Then they went into the store and after a long wait at customer services they were told that no one had handed in a phone. Petra filled in some forms and the assistant said they would let them know if a phone was found.

On the way home it sunk in. She had no phone. They had no landline in the flat. There had been no need as she and her dad both had mobiles. She instantly felt out of touch. Tina seemed miles away suddenly, unreachable. She pictured the streets that led from her house to Tina's and judged it a long way, a fifteen-minute walk at least. Then she thought of Zofia. She'd texted her several times since the previous Sunday. They had all been short and light-hearted, as if the fight with her dad had never happened. That's why she'd sent the card. So that she could say something *meaningful*. Now she wouldn't be able to text her. When they got near home she heard her dad say, 'I might be owed a bit of cash at the weekend; I'll buy you a new phone.'

She mumbled her thanks and helped to carry the shopping up to the flat.

At home she made herself a toasted cheese sandwich and then had some ice cream straight from the tub. After watching some television she went to bed. She woke up at 2.09 a.m. The light was on in the hallway. She guessed her dad was still up. She turned over and pulled the duvet up over her eyes. She tried to go back to sleep but in the back of her head she could hear the sound of whispering voices. Two voices. She sat up.

She went over to her door and opened it as quietly as she could, moving her ear to the gap. It was a male voice. It sounded like Nathan Ball. She huffed. She didn't like that man. She was about to go back to bed when the level of whispering rose and the words became more concerted, like pistons. She strained to listen. Her dad was hardly speaking, it was all Nathan Ball.

'You're just not getting it done! You said you would and it's not happening.'

'I need more time!' Her dad's voice sounded tired, weary.

'I introduced you to Mr Constantine because of your connection to Merchant. You got the chauffeur work because I wanted him to meet you, to trust you. It's been weeks now and Mr Constantine expects you to deliver. He's been patient but twenty thousand pounds is a lot of money. It's owed to him.'

'I know.'

'You said you could get it from Merchant.'

'I said I could try to find out where he keeps his money.'

'Mr Constantine has told you. There's a loose panel in the wall behind an old red velvet chair. Merchant is a simple bloke. Not much imagination. That's where he's always kept the money that he didn't want the authorities to know about.'

'I can't go pulling bits of his wall apart. The room's been changed around. He's disabled. Whenever I go in there I have a look. I'll find it soon but I can't rush it or it'll look suspicious.'

'Mr Constantine is going back to Greece next Friday. He wants the money back by then. He says if you can't find it without alerting the old man then you need to persuade him to tell you where it is. Don't forget there's money in this for you. Plenty of money!'

'I will find it.'

'If you don't get it by Thursday I'm going round there and I'll sort it out. And it won't be nice for the old boy.'

'I'll get it!'

'I'm off. Make sure you keep in touch with me.'

Light from the living room spilt into the hall and Petra stepped back into her bedroom and shut the door. She heard Nathan Ball's footsteps and then the bang of the front door closing. The sound of the television came on and she went back to bed and lay there for a long time, unable to sleep. She stared into the darkness, thinking over the things she'd just heard. There was money in Mr Merchant's house. Money that was owed to Mr Constantine, the man her dad had been driving around. Her dad was supposed to get it in some way. She folded her arms across her chest, feeling let down. Her dad had pretended to be a Good Samaritan, bringing treats for Mr Merchant. He visited him regularly and had told her stories about the old house and the ghostly goings-on. He'd described Mr Merchant as a 'lonely old geezer' and a 'sad old bloke with no family'. But he didn't think those things at all. He'd just gone there because someone else had asked him to find some money for them. He was following orders for Nathan Ball and Mr Constantine, whoever he was.

She remembered what he'd said to her earlier: *I might be owed a bit of cash at the weekend. I'll buy you a new phone.*

It would be bought with cash that came from Mr Merchant's house; money that had been taken from the loose panel of wood behind the red velvet chair. Now, in her mind, her lost phone was somehow linked to the old man in the house that she had once felt mesmerised by. The house with the ghosts who rattled around on the upper floor where no one lived. In reality it was a lonely place where Mr Merchant sat in one room, day after day, with only carers coming in. Her dad dropped by, of course, bringing cigarettes, and looking out for hidden money.

After Sunday she hadn't thought her dad could let her down any more.

But this was a new low. Why was he like this?

When her gran had been alive it hadn't mattered. Her dad had been a little distant in those days. He'd lived in gran's house with her but he'd always been out at work or with friends or sleeping. He'd often go out on a Friday and not come back until Monday morning and her gran would roll her eyes and say, 'Your dad's on a bender!'

There were other times when he was away for weeks or even longer and her gran said that he'd gone to work on the oil rigs. It had been a lie though, because her dad was in prison. When he came home he seemed delighted to see her and took her out to McDonald's, but soon it went back to normal. Her dad and her gran arguing, her dad giving Petra alcohol-fuelled kisses and hugs. Her dad was her *dad* but they didn't spend much time together. It didn't matter though because she had Gran. Gran doted on Petra. She had a sewing machine and would make any clothes that Petra asked for. Petra had asked for Disney characters, not just for her but for Tina as well, and Gran had sat herself down, a bunch of pins in the side of her mouth, and got on with it.

Gran made Dad's meals and washed his clothes. She argued with him and sometimes her dad got angry and shouted at her and punched the wall. Then Gran took his money, saying she needed it for food and rent. 'I'll be skint,' her dad always said.

'Spend a bit less time in the pub,' her gran replied, standing her ground, staring up at him.

She was only fifty-two when she died.

It was an aneurism: a bulging blood vessel in her brain. It happened one evening. She went into the living room to watch *Emmerdale* as Petra was making herself some toast. A while later, when Petra had brushed the crumbs away and rinsed the plate and the butter knife, she'd gone into the living room and found her slumped across the sofa.

It was the worst moment of her life. Petra instantly knew she was dead. The theme tune from *Emmerdale* was playing quietly and the room was absolutely still. She sensed that her gran's life had slipped away from her: her voice, her smile, her laughter; all gone, all finished. She stepped forward and touched Gran's shoulder, a choking sob stuck in her throat.

Then it was just her and her dad.

They moved out of her gran's house to a flat and her dad got a regular job with a cab firm. Petra's life carried on, even though sometimes it felt there was a part of her that was missing: a tiny hole pierced through her chest that no one else could see. Her dad had visits from social workers. There was talk of Petra going into foster care but her dad wouldn't hear of it. She'd looked at him in awe then. It was the first time in a long time that she felt a surge of *love* for him. He promised to care for her, to make sure she got to school and did her homework. The social workers kept talking about his 'haphazard lifestyle' but he brushed it away and said he'd change. They had meetings and would turn up at odd times but she and her dad kept on living together in the flat. It was all going well. Until the weekend when her dad went out and didn't come back for two days.

Petra sat up in bed, her knees making a tent of the duvet. She stared into the darkness of her room. She could hear the low volume of the television. Maybe her dad would fall asleep on the sofa and then in the morning he would wake up with a crick in his neck.

The weekend when her dad fell apart was three months after her gran died. It was when Petra had still been at primary school. She'd come in on the Friday afternoon and found a note to say that he'd got an airport job and might be late. He often left her little notes and she usually watched television and waited for him. As it was Friday they would have a takeaway: a pizza or some fried chicken. But her dad didn't come home that night. She slept on the sofa. The next morning she went round to see Tina but she didn't tell her anything about her dad. It was a normal Saturday and in her head she thought he would come in sometime saying he'd got drunk and stayed at a friend's. When she got home and he wasn't there she was worried. She didn't know what to do. She couldn't call their social worker because then her dad would get in trouble for leaving her. She might end up in foster care. For a while she wondered if he might have been ill or had an accident. She'd seen him come into her gran's once on a crutch, his foot bandaged where he'd fallen down some stairs.

She decided to wait. She bought chips and put the telly on and for a second night she slept on the sofa.

The next day, in the afternoon, he came home. He slumped into the hallway, leaning against one of the walls. She could smell the alcohol from him. Every time he moved it seemed to waft out of him. He mumbled something and made his way to his bedroom and lay face down on the bed, in his clothes. He seemed to go to sleep immediately. Later, during the evening, he came out of his room and looked at her sheepishly. She didn't say anything to him, she just kept her eyes on the television programme. He sat down in the armchair, his elbows on his knees. He looked fidgety, his legs moving up and down.

'Sorry, Petra,' he said.

All of a sudden she couldn't speak. She was filled up with emotion. The worry of the last two days clamped around her throat. She couldn't even look at him. Somewhere among everything else there was anger. He left her alone! What if something had happened to her? What would he say then?

'All right, Petra?'

She kept her face turned away from him. Her only movement was the blink of her eye. She stared at the screen, her eyes blurring.

'I need a drink,' he said and stood up.

That was it. That was the extent of his apology. She swivelled round and watched him go. From the kitchen she heard him opening and closing cupboard doors. He was looking for a bottle of vodka that she'd seen on the shelf that morning. He wouldn't find it because she'd poured it away and taken the bottle down to the recycling bin. She walked out to the kitchen and watched him.

'I don't think you should drink any more,' she said, her voice trembling.

He was still wearing the clothes he'd gone out in on Friday. His jacket and trousers were wrinkled. He spun round to her.

'I got rid of the vodka,' she said.

He looked at her in disbelief.

'What?'

'I didn't want you to drink it.'

'Who do you think you are? Just a kid! You don't tell me what to do.'

'Gran said that you drank too much . . .'

He stepped across to her. She closed her lips tight as if she might stop herself saying anything else. He seemed to loom over her. She could smell him. The fumes of the drinks he'd swallowed in the last two days and nights hit her. She felt nauseous.

'Where is it, miss?' he said, his voice cracking.

'It's gone. It's down the sink.'

'You stupid . . . You stupid . . .'

'You left me on my own,' she said, her voice rising, querulous.

He turned away, mumbling to himself. He had the heels of his hands on his forehead and was shaking his head as if trying to get rid of some thought that was inside it.

'If Gran knew you'd left me . . .' she said weakly.

'Shut up!'

160

'Gran would never . . .'

'SHUT UP!'

He grabbed her by the top of her arm and thrust her out of the kitchen.

'Don't touch my drink,' he said. 'Don't ever touch my drink ever again.'

His fingers were digging into her skin as he manhandled her up the hallway. With one foot he kicked open her bedroom door and propelled her into the room. She lost her footing and hit the side of the wardrobe with a thud, her forehead knocking onto the corner of the wood. She saw stars and staggered back. Then it went black, as if the light had been snatched away. When she opened her eyes again she was on the floor and her dad was looking down at her with fear on his face. She tried to raise her head but it felt heavy like a beanbag.

He took her to A & E.

She'd passed out for a few moments so she had to see a doctor, he said. She could tell them that she'd tripped and fallen over, he said, because in a way that was what had happened. He was only taking her to her room after all, he hadn't meant for her to actually *hurt* herself. He called one of his mates to come and pick them up and then soon after they were sitting in A & E. She felt like she had a big headache, but worst of all was the feel of his fingers at the top of her arm. She glanced down and saw the marks. It had hurt. It still hurt.

The doctors sent for the social worker and she was kept in hospital for two nights. When she was allowed home the flat had been cleaned and her dad and two social workers were there. Her dad hadn't been well, they said, and he'd agreed to go and see a counsellor. He would not be drinking and he would certainly never lay a finger on her again. They would call in twice a week and she was to contact them at any time. They bustled out of the flat, leaving cards with phone numbers on, and when they'd gone her dad had stood up and asked her if she wanted sausages for tea. And crinkle-cut chips.

She'd thought, after going to A & E, that everything would be all right.

But her dad was always good at disappointing her.

Twenty

She watched the house on Princess Street all week.

Every day of the half-term holiday she made it her business to pass it half a dozen times. On the way to Tina's she stopped and looked in at the garden. On the way out to the shops she'd find some excuse to drag Tina and Mandy over to it, all the time keeping an eye out for the angry next-door neighbour. On her way home from Tina's she would see if maybe her dad's cab was there. The newsagent's shop was a good place to stand and stare. Or she simply walked up and down the street, passing it like a guard on duty. She seemed to forget everything else in her life. Zofia's departure to Poland slipped to the back of her mind and she thought only about her dad and wondered what he was going to do and whether there was anything she could do to stop it.

She wanted to tell Tina but Mandy was always around. Another part of her didn't want to tell anyone because it was like opening a box where everything might pour out, not just his plan to rob an old man but the *way* he was, how quick he was to use his hands to get people to do what he wanted. Tina half knew about it anyway, but how could she tell her the rest?

And the thought of Mandy finding out made her ashamed. Mandy with her mum and dad, her nice bag and highlighter pens. 'My mum and dad are having a Halloween party and you can come for a sleepover if you like!' Mandy would love to know about the cracks in Petra's life. She couldn't be a member of The Red Roses but she could luxuriate in Petra's misery.

She thought of making an anonymous phone call to the police.

How would it help though? If they arrived and there was no sign of trouble then they would dismiss it as a prank. If they got there and found her dad and Nathan Ball threatening the old man they'd arrest them both and then Petra would go into foster care.

She didn't know what to do. So she watched the house. As the days went by she spent more time along Princess Street. She walked up one side and then down the other. She stood at the newsagent's, staring at it. She pretended to look at gardens and cars and still she walked up and down and paused sometimes outside the crumbling house.

She hardly saw her dad. He was working. He left her money every day to buy lunch, to go out with her friends. 'Whatever you do,' he'd said, 'don't go near that Polish bitch.' The vehemence of his words distressed her. She thought about going round and telling Zofia but then decided that there was no point. What could she do? She had no influence on him.

So she continued to view the house on Princess Street. She had no idea what was happening there in the hours when she wasn't looking at it. She didn't know if her dad and Nathan Ball had been inside and found Mr Merchant's money already. Still she stared and loitered and pulled Tina and Mandy past the house.

On Thursday, just before one o'clock, she saw Nathan Ball coming along on the opposite side of the road. She went to walk on but stopped and turned to face the window of the newsagent's where the board with the postcards sat. She stared at cards selling second-hand washing machines and baby buggies and worried about what Nathan Ball was doing in the street.

Then she went inside the shop and bought a can of drink. She stood by the glass door and looked out. She could see that Nathan Ball was in a jeans jacket and had his hands in the pockets as though it were a cold day. He was strolling along as if he had nowhere particular to go. At least it looked like that, but Petra thought it was as if he was *acting* as though he had nowhere to go. He stopped in the middle of the pavement and pulled a packet of cigarettes out of his pocket. As he did it he looked backwards down the street. He turned and gazed in the direction of the newsagent's. He was checking that no one was around. He pulled out a cigarette and put it between his lips. Then he felt around his jeans pockets and pulled out a lighter. He lit the cigarette and continued walking.

He went in through the gate of Mr Merchant's house. He was out of her line of sight so she went outside the shop and moved along a few metres, alongside a post box. She watched him walk up to the front door, ducking past some overgrown bushes. He knocked on the door, then he backed away and looked over at the downstairs window. Petra strained her eyes to see but she couldn't make out anyone at the window. She remembered, for a moment, Mr Merchant waving at *her* through the glass. Nathan Ball edged along to the window and looked in. Then he came out of the garden. His face was heavy with annoyance and he was using his hand to flick off leaves from his clothes. The cigarette was gone and she wondered if he'd dropped it, carelessly, in the long grass. He stood in the street for a few moments and pulled out a mobile phone. He pushed some buttons and started talking. She couldn't hear his voice but his finger was pointing in mid-air and he was flexing his shoulders as if he was arguing with someone. She wondered if it was Mr Constantine or maybe her dad. When he finished he walked off the way he had come.

Her can of drink was almost full but she dropped it into the rubbish bin.

What was he doing?

When she got to Tina's, Mandy was already there. It looked as if she'd been there for a while as there were pages of sketches of The Red Roses. She heard Mandy saying, 'We've been doing this, Petra. Have a look and see what you think.'

Petra glanced at the drawings but really she couldn't be bothered. It was on the tip of her tongue to say, 'I'm not in The Red Roses any more. You two do it!' She didn't though. Tina's mum came in with some sandwiches and bags of crisps and left them on the table.

They spent the afternoon watching a DVD and listening to some music. Petra slipped out once, just after three, supposedly to go home and get a particular CD. She walked up and down in front of the house. The living room window looked still. The house looked calm but there was an air of something bad. The bushes in the garden seemed to bristle and thicken in front of her and the fading roses were swooning, letting their petals peel off in the breeze. It was Thursday: the day Mr Constantine wanted his money. Walking back to Tina's, Petra felt a feeling of foreboding. Something bad was going to happen.

'You've been a long time. Where's the CD?' Mandy said.

'I couldn't find it.'

Both Tina's and Mandy's faces were flushed with the heat of the house. Mandy continued talking about the Halloween party and brought out the Argos catalogue, showing pages of phones. After looking at them they began to flick through and talk about what else they would buy. It was gone five and Petra could stand no more. She told them she needed some air. She suggested they go to the newsagent's. Tina leapt up and grabbed her mum's hoodie from the bannister. Mandy didn't look as though she wanted to go out but she came anyway. All the way to Princess Street Petra heard the chatter between Tina and Mandy from far away, as if she were listening to them from another room. It was getting dark as they walked towards the newsagent's. When she stopped she looked keenly up and down the pavements as if she might find Nathan Ball standing there, lurking around the front garden of Mr Merchant's house.

Instead she saw something else.

A white van was parked across the road from the house and Nathan Ball was sitting in the driver's seat, his phone clamped to his ear. His window was open and his elbow was half out of it. He was staring intently at number fifty-three, his lips moving now and then.

'What do you think, Petra?'

She heard Mandy's whining voice like an annoying insect in her ear.

Why was Nathan Ball there, in a van? To get money from Mr Merchant?

'What?' Petra said sharply to Mandy.

'I just said that maybe you and Tina – The Red Roses – could sing at my mum's Halloween party?'

Petra looked up and down the street. She ought to do something.

'Just after the barbecue, when everyone's eating, you could sing a couple of songs. I could introduce you –'

'I think we should go into the house,' Petra heard herself say. 'We've been talking about it for weeks.'

What she meant was, *I've been talking about it for weeks.*

'The house? What house?' Mandy said, looking put out.

'The old house,' she said, pointing across the street at it, keeping one eye on the white van.

'Now? Why?'

'Yes, now. Right now. The three of us can just slip in and out. There's a key round the back, on a hook by the door. We'll just let ourselves in, have a quick look around and then scoot back out again. Remember, the old man sleeps a lot.'

'That's creepy. Why would we do it?'

Because if we go in there I can tell Mr Merchant some men are going to break into his house. I can tell him to call the police. I don't have to mention my dad. When the police car comes it will keep them away and Thursday will be gone and Mr Constantine will go back to wherever he came from.

168

She said something different.

'To see if it's haunted. Come on. Before we get cold feet.'

She could tell them the truth. Why not? But she looked at Mandy and saw an expression of disdain on her face as though she thought Petra was an idiot. She could also see that Mandy was trying to catch Tina's eye. To pull her into her way of thinking. But Tina would never choose Mandy over her.

Just then there was the sound of an engine starting up. The white van had its indicator light on. Nathan Ball had closed the window and the van was moving away from the pavement. He was leaving. Petra didn't know how to feel about it. Was it a good sign?

'Anyway, it'll be completely dark soon . . .' Mandy said, looking round.

'That's why we should go in now. Get in and out, quickly,' Petra said.

She had to go now, while Nathan Ball was out of the street. She hooked her arm through Tina's. It felt a bit stiff at first but then it yielded. They were both looking at Mandy. If they were quick they could go in and Petra could tell Mr Merchant that someone was going to come and rob him. Then it would be up to him what he did about it. Unless he was asleep. She had no idea what she would do then. A feeling of panic, of time moving too quickly, was worming around inside her. Nathan Ball could come back at any minute.

'Come on,' Petra said, making the decision.

She began to walk in the direction of the house. Tina came along with her, light as a feather. Mandy followed but in a slow way. For every two steps Petra and Tina took Mandy took only one. She seemed to drift off from them, as if they were in two boats and she were floating the other way.

'Aren't you coming?' Petra said.

Mandy shook her head as Petra pulled Tina into the front garden.

'You'd better go home then!' Petra said.

Mandy stood looking as though she'd lost something. Tina gave a little wave and she turned and walked off. Petra watched her go and felt a moment's satisfaction. Tina looked pained though. Her mum's hoodie hung off her shoulders.

They crept through the front garden, steering wide of the light from the window. Tina held back.

'I'm not sure this is a good idea,' Tina whispered.

'It's fine,' Petra said.

She linked Tina's arm and they walked towards the gate. She wondered if Tina was thinking of the angry neighbour who'd shouted at them. She wanted to say to her, 'It's dark; no one can see us!' but Tina seemed wound up, tight as a spring. She could let her go, tell her to follow Mandy. She didn't need Tina to go with her; she could go in on her own. She almost opened her mouth to say, 'It's OK, you go and keep Mandy company otherwise she'll be in a mood.' It would have given Tina an excuse and she wouldn't feel that she had let Petra down.

But Petra thought of Mandy's face when Tina showed up. She would be pleased and think that Tina chose Mandy over Petra. She would get her talking about The Red Roses or something. While Petra was edging into the dark house with its cobwebs and scuttling mice, Mandy and Tina would be standing in the warm light from the newsagent's.

They got to the gate.

'I really don't fancy going in there!' Tina hissed.

'Come on. It'll be an adventure. We can make up stories about ghosts for Mandy.'

Petra was nervous. Now that she was at the gate, the enormity of what she was about to do hit her. She was going to burst in on an old sick man and tell him that he was in danger. She fiddled with the handle of the gate. It was tight, almost sticky. She wrestled with it, thinking that maybe she *should* turn back. She could make an anonymous phone call to the police. Use one of the payphones in the shopping centre. She almost turned to go when she felt Tina's hands push hers away as she grasped the handle and wrenched it open.

Tina said, 'Ta dah!'

Petra pushed the gate open and they both went through.

PART THREE: The Present

Mandy

Twenty-One

Mandy was waiting for the counsellor, Debbie Howard. She was in a coffee bar on Holloway Road. She had a drink in front of her which she hadn't touched. While she was waiting she looked, for the hundredth time, at the postcard that had been sent to her almost two weeks before. Her eyes travelled across it. The picture was the kind you might see on a calendar or a greetings card: just a vase of red roses. Mandy's finger had traced a path across the vase and touched each of the flowers, trying to find some meaning in them. Then there were the words on the other side: 'Please don't tell anyone that you saw me. I will contact you.' No signature, no other sign of the sender, and yet Mandy knew exactly who had written it.

She looked up and saw Debbie coming into the coffee shop. She was closing an umbrella up and shaking droplets of water around. She came straight across, leaving her wet umbrella by the chair.

'I'll get a drink and join you,' she said. 'Won't be a minute.'

Debbie was wearing black clothes again: black jeans and a leather jacket. This was their fourth meeting in two weeks and each time she had worn black. Mandy wondered, for a second, if Debbie could be in mourning for something or perhaps it was just a look she had. Mandy watched as Debbie talked to the woman serving her coffee. Debbie was easy to talk to but this would be their fourth time together and Mandy didn't really know what to make of her. Mandy pictured Tommy sitting here at the table, chatting amiably to Debbie, his rock-hard briefcase on the floor next to Debbie's collapsing umbrella. They would get on, Mandy knew; they would have tons of stuff to talk about. It made her feel momentarily weak with jealousy and she pulled herself up straight, took a drink from her cup and tried to fix a smile back on her face.

'How are you?' Debbie said breathlessly, placing a tall cup on the table and a single sachet of sugar next to it.

'I'm good.'

Mandy watched as Debbie shook the sachet rigorously then tore one corner before pouring it into the drink (black coffee as well as black clothes). Then she reached into her bag and pulled out a notepad and pen.

'What have you been up to?' she said while flicking through the pages.

'This and that. Usual things. School, home, school.'

'Mm . . .'

Debbie had found the right page and was sitting looking at Mandy. Her hair tumbled over her shoulders and, as if suddenly aware of this, she used her hands to pull it rigorously back behind her ears. Then she let it go and it fell forward again.

'So, last time we talked a bit about the weeks that led up to your friends' disappearance and I made some notes. I also spoke to my supervisor and she's pointed me in the direction of some recent literature on guilt . . .'

Debbie continued talking about guilt. She kept flicking through her notebook. Mandy thought of Dr Shukla and the notes she had. She remembered the picture on the wall in Dr Shukla's surgery, the one called *Automat* which showed a young woman sitting in a café in the dead of night drinking from a cup. Mandy glanced around at the tables and booths and wondered what it would be like to sit in this café in the early hours of the morning, to look out on the dark street and see the city at night. Then, thinking of the street at night, she pictured Petra emerging from a car in the early hours of the morning, visiting the house that she'd once disappeared from. She'd stood by the wire and gazed at the remains of the property like a ghost. As soon as Petra heard her name being called she faded back into the car in which she had come.

'You look as though you're miles away!'

Debbie was staring at her. She was right. Mandy's thoughts had travelled a long way. That was how it was lately: she found it hard to concentrate on one thing for very long.

'Sorry, I've got a lot on my mind.'

'Yes. That's why we're here. OK, so where were we? Maybe you could go through those early weeks of the school term again, focusing on your friendship with the two girls.'

Mandy talked again about the events of the first seven weeks at secondary school when she got together with Petra and Tina. Debbie made notes in the pad. Every now and then she asked her something but then went back to writing. When Mandy had said all she could think of, Debbie closed the pad with a flourish. The man behind the counter was gazing over at them. Mandy wondered if he was put out by two people clearly using his café as a meeting room, but Debbie had said she'd done it with other patients. 'It's important to get out of a clinical setting and just talk,' she'd said.

'I've had some thoughts, Mandy, which I've shared with my supervisor . . .'

The word 'supervisor' made Mandy think of a boss, but the supervisor in this case was the professor who was overseeing Debbie's PhD thesis.

'And she suggested that I read up some studies, in particular American cases . . .'

'You mean like the Cleveland girls? The three who were kidnapped and held for ten years . . .'

'No, not that. No . . .' Debbie looked a touch flustered. 'No, she suggested I look at some studies of teenage girls who were suffering from depression because of feelings of exclusion. I think some of these may have some relevance to your case.'

'I don't understand.'

Debbie flicked through her notebook and stopped at a page crammed with writing. She read for a moment and Mandy felt frustration building. She'd agreed to these meetings because the counsellor was from outside, not someone she'd seen before. But the sessions hadn't produced anything new. It had been Debbie asking the same old questions and her telling the same old story. Now she was going to tell her she was depressed? She knew that!

'If we divide up the events of five years ago there are three strands. Firstly, your friendship with the two girls, secondly, you refused to go into the house with the two girls and thirdly, you told no one where they went for five hours.'

Mandy was interested now. It had never been put to her like this before.

'Let's start with the third one: you told no one about the girls going into the house. This is clearly an action you took that had grave consequences. You were twelve years old and your reasons were clear. You didn't want to get into trouble. It was not the case that you thought, *I know Petra and Tina are in that house and I know that something terrible is happening to them but I'm not going to tell anyone.* No, you simply did what most people do and looked out for yourself.'

It sounded bald, hard, selfish. Mandy glanced round, afraid that someone might hear Debbie, but no one was nearby. Behind the counter the man was intent on polishing the veneer of the coffee machine, making small circles with a cloth.

'Let's look at the second point,' Debbie said. 'You refused to go into the house with the two girls. I want you to consider this. Are you feeling bad about this because you let them down in some way? Perhaps you feel that you should have gone with them, as part of the group. Or maybe you feel that you should have persuaded them not to go and that gives you pain.'

Mandy thought about this. Had she felt anything specific about them going into the house without her? Normally her feelings seemed like one tight ball but now she was being asked to pull them apart, like peeling petals from a closed flower.

'Lastly, let's look the first point: your friendship with the two girls. You spent the time leading up to the tragedy trying to be part of this friendship group, and there are things that

179

you've said, certainly to Dr Shukla in the past, that indicate that you were aggrieved that they did not accept you with open arms. I want to suggest that a big part of the pain – the depression – you are feeling may be to do with this unresolved feeling of rejection from these two girls. Or at least from one of these girls – *Petra*. This is why, I believe, it was *Petra* you thought you saw on the bus those times. Tina, who did accept your friendship and was warm towards you, does not haunt you in the way Petra does. When I say "haunt", I'm speaking metaphorically.'

Mandy sat back in her chair and folded her arms. She didn't answer. Her sense of frustration had gone and she was thinking about what Debbie had said. She'd always wondered why it was Petra she saw those times and not Tina. Could it be that she was unhappy because of Petra's rejection of her? What sort of person did that make her though? That she was more upset about her own hurt feelings than the fact that two girls had disappeared?

'I just want you to think about these things for me. You have a lot of hurt inside you. What we have to do is isolate the things that we can mend.'

'What about the things we can't mend?'

'You have to find a way to live with those. You were twelve years old. If those girls are indeed dead, as everyone thinks they are, then you have to understand that it was not *you* who killed them.'

Debbie closed her book and slid it into a pocket in her bag. She stirred the rest of her coffee before drinking it down in one go.

'I have to make a move,' she said, picking up her umbrella and fussing with the flaps. 'I have a lecture to go to. But I'll see you after school on Thursday? Same time, same place?'

Mandy watched her leave the café. She thought, for a moment, how detached Debbie seemed, as if none of the emotions ever affected her. Maybe this was the reason Mandy felt comfortable with her. She was tired of wallowing in feelings; she wanted answers and Debbie seemed able to give them to her. Through the window she saw her put up the umbrella and walk off. Then she sat for a while with her hands around the cup even though her drink was finished.

If those two girls are dead as everyone thinks they are . . .

Now there was another problem. One she couldn't tell Debbie about. One of the two girls was not dead, Mandy knew. She had seen her with her own eyes. It was no manifestation of her own guilt, it was the real-life person of Petra. And she had received a postcard from her. 'I will contact you,' it said. That had been two weeks ago.

Mandy was waiting for that contact: a call, a letter, another glimpse of Petra.

She was still waiting.

Twenty-Two

Mandy had a text from Jon Wallis.

Got something re that girl you asked about.

All day Mandy looked for him. He wasn't in the sixth-form common room and a couple of the boys she spoke to said he was coming in late. They also gave her a suggestive look when she asked them what time he was due in. She ignored it, pretending she didn't understand what it was they were implying. At lunchtime she went to the dining hall and scanned the room to see if he was at one of the tables. Then she left the school site and walked to the local shops and café that a lot of the kids used. He was nowhere to be seen.

She sent him three texts all asking him to find her asap.

She had history in the afternoon and she deliberately got there late so that she could sit in the seat nearest the door and not have the choice to sit by Tommy. He waved across at her and she smiled at him and got on with taking notes. He must have known that she was avoiding spending time with him. Returning to school after the half-term she'd said, 'I'm so behind on assignments, I'm going to be stuck in the library for most of this week!' He'd given her a sympathetic expression but she'd caught his eye as he did it and in that moment she knew that he understood. She'd felt her face warm up and flustered through a list of things she had to complete but his look had told her everything. He'd *known* how she felt about him. He knew why she was shying away from him.

She'd seen him and Leanne in the common room on the first morning back. They sat together and Leanne whispered things in his ear, her mouth almost touching his skin. Leanne looked her usual doll-like self, her hair hanging down over one shoulder. Even though the weather had turned cold she was still wearing short sleeves and a light jacket, which meant she did a lot of shivering. Later that day Mandy had seen her walking around with one of Tommy's jumpers draped over her shoulders, the arms tied together, the cuffs hanging over her breasts.

She didn't hate Leanne. She was just angry with herself for not realising the kind of girl that Tommy wanted. Not someone like Mandy. When she bumped into Tommy alone in the corridor or outside a classroom they fell into their old chatter, talking about films and books, but later when she saw him with his arm around Leanne it gave her a gnawing pain.

After history Mandy had a free period and went to the library. She found a carrel and placed her books open in front of her so that it looked as though she were hard at work. It wasn't long before her mind went back to Petra and the fact that it was two weeks and one day since she'd been contacted. Every day she'd woken up and wondered if this was to be the day when she got a phone call or a message of some sort from her. She felt it keenly when she was out somewhere, sure that Petra would approach her then. She pictured herself walking along Holloway Road and being called at by someone across the way, or perhaps if she was in a sandwich shop choosing something for lunch there would be a tap on her shoulder and Petra would be there standing behind her and Mandy would say, 'My God, Petra, I thought you were dead.' But fifteen days had gone by without a word and now Mandy began to think that she wouldn't hear anything from her at all. Her appearance at the house over two weeks ago would be as much a mystery as her disappearance at that very same house five years before.

Was there anything Mandy could do? She knew what she had seen. She had the postcard. Should she go to the police? Find Officer Farraday and talk to him? He would think she was mad though, especially when she described going to the demolition site early in the morning. And Dr Shukla, if asked, would tell them that she had imagined Petra years before and that now she was seeing a counsellor for depression. No one would believe Mandy. Five years ago they wished she'd spoken up, told them where the girls had gone. Now they would wish her to shut up, to keep her imaginings to herself.

She did some work, taking notes on the first scene of *Cat on a Hot Tin Roof*. She read the dialogue and noted down character points. Then she sat with her chin on her hand and gazed round the library. There were some boys from the upper sixth on the computers. The boy she'd asked about Jon Wallis was there and he gave her a knowing look. She turned away, cross. She thought of Jon's text and pulled her phone out to check that he hadn't tried to contact her again. There was no answer to her text. What *was* it that he wanted to tell her? On the day when he'd given her the envelope from Petra she'd quizzed him over and over. 'What did the girl say? Exactly? Word for word? What did she look like? What was she wearing? What about the car she was in?' He'd not really taken any notice, he'd said. She'd walked up and asked him to give the envelope to Mandy Crystal. Then she'd gone back towards a car, a white car, he thought. She was young with shoulder-length reddish hair and was wearing dark trousers and a top that was like a uniform of some sort. That was all he could remember.

'Hi, Mandy,' a voice said.

She turned and saw Lucy standing by the carrel – the girl she'd talked to at Zoe's party. She'd seen her at lunch a couple of days before and they'd chatted for a while, mostly about the poor food. Lucy hadn't alluded to the party or the fact that she knew how upset Mandy had been. Mandy was grateful for that but felt awkward with her. She didn't even know her second name.

'What are you up to?' Lucy said.

'Just taking some notes. Catching up on work.'

'I'm behind too. There's so much reading to do . . .'

'I know.'

Lucy looked around the library, her mouth open as though she was about to talk. Mandy waited, glancing back at her notes, not sure what to say.

'I wondered,' Lucy said, tentatively, 'if you'd like to come

185

over to my house at the weekend? My mum will be there and she said she'd love to show you how to make some earrings.'

'Oh.'

Mandy looked away, at her book, at her notes, embarrassed. Lucy was making an attempt at *friendship*. She had no room in life for a new friend.

'Just for a couple of hours. I live quite near you.'

'That sounds good,' Mandy said, pulling herself together. 'I'll just check with my mum? I'm not sure if she's got plans for the weekend. Can I text you?'

'Sure,' Lucy said.

'Here, write your number down for me.'

Mandy pushed the corner of her notepad over to the edge of the carrel and held out her pen for Lucy. Lucy took it and scribbled her mobile number down.

'See you later,' Lucy said and walked off.

When the library door closed Mandy felt bad. Lucy was being kind, she knew. She probably thought that now Mandy had lost Tommy she had a vacancy for a friend. That was the last thing Mandy wanted. She saw the screen of her phone light up. There was a message from Jon.

I'm in the common room now.

She replied:

Be there soon.

Mandy packed her stuff away and headed off.

Jon Wallis was sitting by the window, looking at his phone. There were other kids around but no one was nearby. When she walked in he looked up and smiled, leaning forward in his chair and placing his phone on the low table in front. His hair looked long, shaggy almost. She was sure he used to keep it short. When had it grown? She hadn't noticed.

'Hi,' she said, putting her bag on the seat beside him and sitting on the next one along.

'How are you?' Jon said.

'OK.'

'I see your best mate has got himself a girlfriend.'

'Yeah . . ' Mandy looked down at her bag; there was dust all over the bottom of it. She brushed it away.

'I thought you and him . . .'

'No, no. Not at all. We're just mates.'

'I thought he was gay, anyway.'

'Why? Because of the way he dresses?'

'No. Well, that too. No, there's something about him.'

'He's not.'

'Don't matter to me whether he is or not. I was just saying.'

'So,' Mandy said, trying to pull the conversation back on track, 'you said you had something to tell me about the girl who gave you the letter for me.'

Jon nodded. Mandy waited.

'There's something I don't get, though,' he said. 'How come you don't know this person? Why would someone you don't know send you a letter via your school?'

187

Mandy frowned. She could feel her face was screwed up because she genuinely didn't know how to answer him. Why hadn't she considered this? That he would be puzzled, intrigued even. She couldn't tell him the truth though. She sighed.

'If I tell you, you have to promise not to say a word to anyone.'

Jon leant forward, his face rapt with curiosity. She lowered her voice, even though there was no one nearby to hear them.

'That letter? It was an anonymous note about the missing girls. I don't know if it's a fake or a joke or what. I don't want to take it to the police in case it means nothing and gets everyone's hopes up. I've had them before, over the years: letters, phone calls about the girls.'

The lies came easily. Jon sat up and assumed a serious expression. This was what happened to most kids she knew whenever she mentioned 'the girls'. It was shorthand for years of sadness and loss. Kids always seemed to stiffen up, look at her in a kindly but distant way. It was why she'd clicked with Tommy so quickly. He'd reacted differently.

'So if I could find out who this person was who gave the envelope to you then I could work out how genuine it was . . .'

'Right. Well, I won't say a word to anyone,' he said. 'So, yesterday, we went on a trip to the British Museum. We were doing some primary research, looking at old manuscripts. It was pretty good as it goes . . .'

'Yes?' Mandy said.

'Anyway, a few of us went out for a walk around at lunchtime and I saw this car parked on a double yellow line and half up on the pavement. It was a car – not a van – and on the back, on the hatch window, it had some italic writing. It was for cakes. I wrote it down here.'

Jon pulled something out of his trouser pocket. It was a scrap of newspaper, the corner of a page that had been torn off. On the margin was some handwriting. He read it out.

'"Paris Patisserie. We deliver to your door." There's a phone number as well.'

She didn't say anything, unsure as to what he was offering her.

'As soon as I saw the car and the writing on the back I felt as if I'd seen it somewhere before. Then I remembered. It was on the back of the car that the girl got into. The one who gave me the letter for you. It was the word "Patisserie" that I noticed because it's unusual.'

'Did you see the girl again?'

'No, the car was empty. Maybe they were delivering stuff. I don't know. But I thought I'd tell you. It would be easy to look on the web and find out where the shop is.'

'Yes,' Mandy said.

'Then you could go and ask around. See who worked there. Unless it's a huge place you should be able to spot her. Do you want me to come with you? I could come along, if you felt nervous about going on your own.'

Mandy was surprised. It was the second time that day she'd been offered some sort of friendship. The last one she'd all but turned down. She had no intention of taking anyone with her to find Petra but she didn't want to sound ungrateful.

'Maybe. Or maybe, after I've been to check it out, we could have a coffee. A way of me saying thank you.'

Jon nodded. 'Send me a text.'

He slid his phone off the table, picked his bag up and left. She sat there for a few moments, looking at the scrap of newsprint in her hand. *Paris Patisserie*. Now she wouldn't have to wait any longer for Petra to contact her.

Twenty-Three

Paris Patisserie was not a shop. It was a bakery based in Kentish Town. Mandy found its website easily and read over the services it offered. 'We travel all over North London providing patisserie for all functions and events. We deliver regularly to offices, cafés and conference centres. We will also supply our premium products for special events: weddings, parties, birthdays and work-related celebrations. You can order through our website or by phone.' The website had photographs of a wide range of pastries and gateaux with prices and details alongside them. There were smiling chefs and pictures of a van and a car, and also a moped, similar to those used by pizza delivery firms. The italicised logo was on the side of the van and the moped but it was on the back window of the car as Jon Wallis had said.

Mandy put the postcode into Google Maps. It showed a minor road a couple of streets away from Kentish Town tube station. She would go there tomorrow instead of school. She was not sure what she would do when she got there but she would at least see where it was and whether there was any sign of the girl with the red hair who she thought (almost certainly) was Petra.

She heard the doorbell from downstairs. Her mother shouted, 'I'll get it.'

She tidied her books up and thought about Jon Wallis and his offer to go with her to the shop. She'd been touched by it. She'd known he liked her for a while. He lived ten or so houses along her street, although when she was in the lower forms he largely ignored her. He was one of the older boys she saw around, too disdainful to speak to anyone younger. After she'd done her GCSEs he changed and became friendly towards her, sometimes walking along with her when she was leaving school. He told her what it was like in the sixth form and said that she could hang out with him and his mates any time if she wanted to. She'd been flattered and might have taken him up on his offer if Tommy hadn't breezed into school and swept her up into his company. Jon Wallis was chatty and easy-going but Tommy had a spark that just drew people to him. It didn't work with everyone though. Anyone who was extroverted with their clothes and their personality was looked on with suspicion by the long line of sixth-form boys who liked their football teams and their music and their video games. Boys like Jon didn't *get* people like Tommy. Tommy was interested in books and art and movies. He liked to argue about politics and philosophy and was proud of the oddness of his clothes.

Tommy was unique.

Mandy sat down on the edge of her bed and felt herself go weak. Tommy was who she *wanted*. Not Jon Wallis. Not Lucy (whatever her surname was). But Mandy was not for him. He wanted one of the girly girls.

She heard footsteps up the stairs and then her room door opened slightly. Her mum peeked in.

'Alison's here. I'm just making her a cup of tea. Come down and say hello.'

Mandy sighed. 'I've got loads of work . . .'

Her mum looked round her room. Her bag was on the floor, her school things not yet unpacked. Her laptop was open though, showing the website for Paris Patisserie. She shut it down guiltily.

'Looks to me like you're wasting time on Facebook. Just come down for five minutes. You've not seen Alison since she came back from France. Please! You know how she likes to talk to you!'

Mandy nodded stiffly and her mum went back downstairs. She closed her eyes in irritation. Why did she always have to be present when Alison came? She was tired of trying to be positive in front of her, especially now that she had all this stuff about Petra in her head. How could she look Alison in the face when her mind was full of Petra? She could imagine Alison staring at her with her sharp eyes and suspecting the contents of Mandy's thoughts.

Seeing Alison had always been an ordeal and she was tired of being an audience for her suffering. The trip to France had come to nothing. The girl at the garage had turned out not to be Tina at all. She was a girl from a group of travellers who were staying in the area for a short time. Alison had spent five days there. She had liaised with police and other traveller's sites had been checked. She had been interviewed by French television and had also met parent support groups of missing

French children. When she first got back she was interviewed by one of the breakfast news programmes. She seemed calm and articulate: 'We have to follow up every lead, no matter how fragile.' Mandy had watched for a few moments before changing channels. Alison had dark lipstick on and her skin was pale. She looked slick and in control and yet Mandy was sure that when she raised her hand to make a point it was trembling, as if all her emotions had been pushed out to the tips of her fingers.

Where is Tina? Alison must ask that question every hour of every day.

Mandy had asked it too. Where was Tina? If Petra *was* working in a bakery in Kentish Town then *where was Tina?*

She could hear her mum calling her. She went to the door of her room.

'Mandy! The tea's ready. Come and have a cup.'

Mandy didn't answer. Then she heard another voice.

'Mandy, come and see me. I'll tell you about my trip to France!' Alison called.

She sighed and went downstairs.

Mandy found the bakery within minutes of getting to Kentish Town Tube station the next morning. She walked along a busy road then turned off onto a cul-de-sac which ended after a number of shops and houses. Opposite was a warehouse with a high wire fence. At the very edge of it was a brick building that looked as though it had once been a primary school. There was a large sign with a variety of business headings and down at the bottom Mandy could see 'Paris Patisserie'. There were solid iron gates and alongside them an entry-pad with a speaker. Inside, in what used to be the playground, Mandy could see a number of parked vehicles and in among them was the Paris Patisserie van and car. As she stood there a couple of men emerged from a door in the building. They were wearing white trousers and tops and were taking a cigarette break. She wondered if they worked for Paris Patisserie or one of the other companies that used the premises.

She turned away from the building and thought about what to do. Across the road was a café. She walked towards it and decided to spend some time there thinking about how to proceed. Five minutes later she was sitting by the window with a cup of black coffee, staring out at the entrance to the old primary school.

She might have to sit there all day.

There was no guarantee that she would see Petra going into work or coming out. It might be her day off. She might not even work there regularly. If she *was* one of the people who delivered the pastries she may get picked up from her home address and then go round the offices and shops making calls. She might never come to this building. Mandy could sit there for a week and not see her.

That's if it even was Petra. It was a stupid idea to come.

And yet five minutes later, before Mandy's coffee had cooled enough for her to take a sip, a girl with red hair came out of the building and walked towards the iron gates. Mandy stared at her, unable to believe her eyes. She was wearing a short green puffa jacket and jeans. Her hair was parted at the side, sleek and straight, and sat on her shoulders. It was the colour of mahogany. She stood at the gate for a second before a small door opened within it and she stepped outside onto the street. Mandy stood up, picked up her bag and left her coffee on the table. She paused in the doorway of the café to allow the girl with red hair (was it Petra?) to walk ahead. She headed after her just as the girl turned the corner onto the high street. Mandy followed, keeping well back. The green puffa jacket stood out and she was able to see her from a distance. She hoped she didn't get a bus or a Tube. After a short while the girl stopped and went into a shop. Mandy paused as if looking at some posters on a wall nearby. She glanced up in the direction of the shop that the girl had gone into. She came out of it carrying what looked like a large container of milk. Mandy continued to follow her. It wasn't long before she turned off the high street. She was heading down a road with houses tightly packed on each side. Mandy slowed up, feeling a flutter of excitement. Was this where she was staying? Could it be this easy to find her?

The girl turned into a front garden then knocked at the door. Mandy could hear the *thump thump* of the knocker. The door opened and then shut. Mandy crossed the road and walked on until she was opposite. Number thirty-four. It had a FOR SALE sign in the front garden and looked a bit run-down.

What was she going to do?

Mandy walked along a bit, her confidence failing her. Was this the right person? She'd seen her face properly once, in the beam of light that came from a torch. She'd called her by her name and then she'd received the postcard via Jon Wallis. Surely it *was* Petra. What was she going to say to her? *Where have you been for five years? Where is Tina?*

Another feeling wormed its way around inside her. She hated herself for even thinking these thoughts. She had never been Petra's choice of friend. Petra had always been a reluctant participant in the threesome, sometimes barely hiding her contempt for Mandy. Hadn't she done the exact same thing *now*? After having been seen by Mandy she'd asked her not to tell anyone and said that she would contact her. But she hadn't. Maybe, like five years ago, she couldn't bear to have Mandy in her life again.

Mandy scrabbled at her wrist but there was no bangle for her to worry at. She was out of her depth here. She thought of Alison Pointer. She would do anything to find Tina and maybe the same went for Petra. Surely Petra was the key to knowing where Tina was, if she was still alive. Perhaps, now that she had the address, she should tell Alison or at the very least go to the police. Let them ask the girl with the red hair some questions.

The front door of the house opened and two men came out. They were talking loudly in a foreign language and one of them was laughing and clapping the other on the back. They walked off up the street.

Mandy didn't know what to do.

She thought about the counsellor, Debbie. The last time she saw her she'd told her that one of the reasons for her continuing unhappiness was the unresolved hurt she felt about being rejected by Petra. Was this what was stopping her going across to the house, lifting the heavy knocker and demanding to see her now? She found herself slumping against the garden wall behind her. She'd lost impetus. She'd become weak. She

197

imagined Petra opening the door and giving a sigh. 'You again!' she might say. 'Can't you get your own friends? Do you have to be always hanging round with me?'

Maybe Tommy thought that about her. Perhaps he saw her as too needy and that was why he went for Leanne. Was this always going to be Mandy's problem? That she needed people too much?

There was a face at the downstairs window of the house. It was not the girl with the red hair but a woman. She was looking straight across the road at Mandy, making no attempt to hide herself behind the curtain. She was *staring* at her, no, more than that; she was glaring at her as if she was angry.

Mandy walked across the street. In moments she was standing at the front door and picking up the knocker, letting it bang loudly on the door. The door opened and the same woman stood there. She was small and had her hair pulled right up on the top of her head. She had attitude – her shoulders squared, her neck stretched, her face piqued, ready to argue, to tell Mandy to get lost.

'I want to speak to Petra,' she said.

'Petra?' the woman said with a tiny shake of her head as if Mandy had said, 'I want to speak to Father Christmas.'

'I know she's in there. I need to speak to her. Petra Armstrong.'

'You have wrong address!' the woman said, her accent foreign, her words heavy like planks of wood being piled against her.

'I know she's here. I saw her. She sent me a postcard. I need to speak to her otherwise I'll go to the police!'

'No one here of that name. No one. Is house full of Polish. We don't know Petra.'

'OK, I'll call the police then.'

Mandy took her phone out of her pocket. She was desperate and had no idea what she was doing, but she pressed nine once and then a second time. Before she pressed it again a voice called out from inside the house.

'It's OK. I'll speak to her.'

The woman turned round. There, at the end of the hallway, was Petra.

Twenty-Four

Mandy stood on the doorstep. Petra walked up the hallway towards her. Mandy was holding her breath, her eyes travelling up and down this girl who she had once known. She was tall, thin and had long reddish hair that was parted at one side. She had on tight jeans and plimsolls and a baggy top. There were several bangles on her wrist and a chain round her neck on which hung a cross. Her face had a grown-up look but still, there, around the features, Mandy could see the younger girl. When she came to the front door she twisted her lips to the side and it was as if Mandy had gone back in time.

Petra spoke to the woman at the door in another language. The woman shrugged her shoulders. Petra put her arm around the woman's shoulder and said softly, '*Bedzie wszystko w porzadku.*' The woman answered rapidly, and Petra listened and nodded, glancing at Mandy from time to time. The woman kept going, speaking in paragraphs. Petra whispered something with one finger up at Mandy as if to say, *I won't be a minute.*

Mandy noticed her nails then. They were silver and long and rested on the woman's shoulder, delicately curved like beads that Mandy might use to make a bangle. She glanced at her own nails, bitten down. She folded her arms, hiding her hands. The woman had stopped speaking and was looking at Mandy in a poisonous way. Then she turned and headed for the stairs. Petra waited until she'd gone up before she spoke.

'What are you doing here?' she said. 'How did you know where I was?'

'Hello, Petra,' Mandy said, ignoring the question.

Petra looked suspiciously at her, as if something had just come into her head. She stepped out onto the doorstep and looked up and down the street.

'You've not brought anyone with you,' she said.

'Brought who?'

'*Policja*,' Petra said. 'The police?'

'You said not to tell anyone and I didn't. You said you would contact me and you didn't. I haven't brought anyone but unless you tell me what happened I will walk straight away from here and ring the police now,' Mandy said.

Petra's eyes were scanning the road behind Mandy.

'I'm not lying. I've been the truthful one so far here. You're the one who lied.'

Petra slumped against the side of the porch. All the tension seemed to run off her.

'I was going to get in touch. If you hadn't turned up today I would have written to you, care of the school. It's been very busy. I've had a lot of work on.'

'Where've you been, Petra?' Mandy said, her voice a hiss. 'The whole country was looking for you. Your dad . . .'

'You need some kind of explanation. It's just that the house is full of people . . .'

201

Just then, as if on cue, the kitchen door opened and a young man poked his head out and called out a name. Petra said something to him but Mandy couldn't understand what it was. The door closed.

'You've changed your name.'

'Of course.'

There it was. The old disdain. Petra's eyes flicking to the side as if illustrating to someone else how stupid Mandy was. She might as well have added 'Duh!' Mandy looked sharply at her, her jaw tensed, her features pointed angrily. Petra immediately closed her eyes and whispered, '*Przepraszam.*' Then she said, 'Sorry,' and put her hand out and touched Mandy's coat sleeve.

'I will tell you but not here. There's a park down the road. You go ahead and I'll come in five minutes.'

'I'm not going anywhere.'

Petra stood very still but there were things going on inside her head; Mandy could tell by the twitches of her mouth and the movement of her eyes.

'I haven't been fair to you,' she finally said, pulling herself together. 'I'll get my coat and we'll both go down to the park. We can talk there.'

She went back into the house, up the stairs where the woman had gone. There was hurried talk; Mandy could hear voices scissoring across each other. Then she came back down wearing the green puffa jacket. It was unzipped and the front was flying apart as Petra came towards her.

Mandy followed her along the street, Petra a couple of paces ahead. It was surreal that this girl could be here; as though she had risen from the dead. When she got to the park she headed for a bench. Mandy joined her.

'Where've you been?' she said, as soon as she sat down, determined to get straight to the point.

The park looked damp and brown and there were piles of leaves drifting up to the bench. Some of the trees were bare and the flower beds had been replanted with winter pansies. The children's play area was empty except for a young girl with a pushchair. A woman on a mobility scooter went past, a dog running alongside her.

'I will explain,' Petra said. 'But first, have you seen my father?'

Mandy nodded, remembering Jason Armstrong at the demolition of the house.

'How is he?'

'Not so good.'

Mandy was holding the edge of the seat. She could feel the wood splintering at her fingers. Why couldn't Petra just speak?

'What happened, Petra? On that night? When you went into the house?'

'It's a simple explanation. Tina and I went in. You knew that. You were there. We hid in the kitchen. It was dark there and the door was ajar so we could see into the living room. Mr Merchant – the old man – was in his chair. Tina was jittery. She hadn't really wanted to go in. She just did it out of loyalty to me.'

This was true.

'Anyway we were only in there for a few moments and Tina was jumpy. I felt her arm and it was rigid, like she'd seized up with fright at what we were doing. She said, "I've got to go."

So I let go of her and gave her a little push towards the door. It was like she needed my permission to leave so I gave it to her. And she went. She left me there. I was a bit miffed and once she'd gone there seemed no point in me staying. I waited a few more minutes; I suppose I thought I might have a look around but I didn't. It was dark and because I was on my own I was scared. I left as well. Tina was nowhere to be seen so I went home.'

'The old man was murdered.'

'I *know*. I read about all this on the internet. Mr Merchant . . .' she said, pausing, '. . . was alive when I left.'

'And Tina . . .'

'I thought Tina had gone home or probably round your house.'

Could it be as simple as that? They both left the house separately?

'I've been blaming myself for not telling anyone that the two of you went into that house for the last five years. And now you're saying that neither of you stayed in there?'

'None of it was your fault.'

'But if I'd said, as soon the police came round . . .'

'If you had told the police straight away it wouldn't have made any difference. Tina had left the house and so had I. Whatever happened to Tina happened outside, on the street, on the way home or on the way to your house. In fact that's where the police started looking, on the streets. You have nothing to feel guilty about.'

Mandy felt herself shift about uncomfortably. This was something that had never occurred to her. That whatever she had done that night wouldn't have made one bit of difference either way.

'You never met my father, did you? Back then?' Petra said.

'I saw him a couple of times.'

'He had a problem with anger. Whenever he got down or unhappy he hit out at someone. My gran, his girlfriends and me, maybe even my mum when she was alive. Social services knew about it. They kept a close eye on his drinking. It wasn't hard for me to live with him. I *wanted* to live with him. The aggression usually only came out when he was drunk. He always said sorry afterwards. Social services had a kind of contract with him. He went to counselling, he kept control of his drinking and he promised not to lay a finger on me. Mostly he managed it. And if he did hurt me then I covered it up and didn't tell anyone. How could I tell? The alternative was foster care and I didn't want that. I *managed* it. I was happy enough. After I lost my gran nothing much mattered to me. Well, except for Tina. Tina was like my sister. That day, that Thursday, my dad had been drinking from the night before and continued during the day. He got really angry with me in the morning and he hit out at me. I had bruises all down one arm and on my ribs. You didn't see them because I covered them up.'

Mandy didn't speak. There had always been something *hidden* about Petra.

'Tina didn't see them either, but she knew I was having a bad time. That night, after I left Mr Merchant's house, I went home. My dad was asleep on the settee and he had a line of beer cans on the floor in front of him and half a bottle of vodka in the kitchen. I was pretty miserable and I couldn't face a night waiting for him to wake up and start throwing his weight around again. So I went and stayed with his ex-girlfriend. I told her that he said it was OK and we watched DVDs and went to bed and woke up late. Then we saw the news and realised what had happened.'

'Why didn't you come forward?'

'Because I knew that that was the end. I was covered in bruises and I'd been missing all night. I'd get sent into foster care.'

'You stayed away for five years to avoid that?'

'I didn't intend to stay away for ever. I – we – took it day by day. I thought the bruises might heal. I had this mad idea that I could go to the police after a couple of days and say I'd lost my memory.'

'What about the girlfriend? Surely she would have made you go to the police.'

'She knew what my dad was like. She cared about me and in any case she had plans to go back to Poland so she wouldn't be a part of it. I was also worried sick about Tina. I thought if I went to the police then the story would get confused. It would be about me when it needed to be about *her*. I had no idea what had happened to her and I kept thinking about all these horrible things. It was a terrible few days.'

'But you didn't go back . . .'

Petra shook her head.

'You went with your dad's ex-girlfriend back to Poland.'

Petra lips pursed. 'I can't say any more. I don't want to get anyone else in trouble. She cared about me. I made the decision that I wanted to be with her and not my dad. As the days went by and there was no explanation about what happened to Tina I realised that if I went back my life was either going to be with my dad or in care and either way I wasn't going to have Tina any more. So it seemed to me that my old life was finished. *Petra Armstrong* was finished, so I made a new start.'

Mandy didn't know what to say. People didn't just make decisions about leaving their old lives behind. *They just didn't.*

'It doesn't sound plausible.'

'I can't help that. It's the truth. I've had a good life. I live with someone who loves me. We are like sisters.'

'But you've come back.'

'Just for a short period for work. We needed some work. The money's good.'

'Weren't you afraid you might be recognised?'

'I've grown up. It's five years now. In any case there are eight million people in London. I was hardly likely to bump into my father.'

'You went to the house. You bumped into me.'

'I did. I didn't expect to see someone there at five o'clock in the morning.'

Mandy felt embarrassed. It was an odd time for someone to be out. She couldn't explain why she'd gone there.

'I was shocked to see the house wasn't there any more. Stunned when I saw you walk out of the shadows.'

A car beep sounded. Mandy looked towards the entrance of the park. There was a car idling by the gates. Standing next to it was the woman who had answered the front door earlier. She was wearing a long coat and she had her arms folded in a belligerent way. Petra stood up and began to fiddle with the zip at the bottom of her jacket, trying to fasten it. She walked a couple of steps. Mandy got up and followed her, taking her arm to stop her going any further.

'You're leaving?'

'Yes.'

'Right now? This minute?'

'I can't take the chance . . .'

'You think I'll tell the police?'

'Would you?'

'I don't know.'

'Mandy, I just can't take that chance.'

Mandy stared at the woman and the car. She imagined hastily packed suitcases in the back of it. That must have been what Petra had said to her in Polish. 'Pack everything and we'll leave,' because Mandy couldn't be trusted.

'You never liked me, did you?' she said.

Petra sighed. 'Not much. I might have got to like you . . .'

'I was lonely. I needed a friend.'

'So you pushed your way between me and my friend,' Petra said, an edge of anger to her voice. 'Tina was everything to me and you prised her away.'

'You were always her number one.'

'Maybe,' she said, softening. 'You spent a lot of time with her during those weeks. She talked about you. I knew she liked you.'

The car beeped again. The woman shouted something towards her.

'What do you think happened to Tina?' Mandy said.

'She must have been taken by someone. I don't think she's alive any more.'

Petra's eyes had glassed over. Mandy pulled Petra towards her. She gave her a clumsy hug and then released her, stepping away.

'I have to go. Goodbye, Mandy. Please don't tell anyone about me.'

Mandy watched Petra walk towards the woman and the car. The woman stood on tiptoes and gave her a hug. They got into the car and moments later it drove off.

Mandy pulled the postcard out of her pocket and thought of The Red Roses. Mandy would have made a good member of the group. Petra had been wrong about that.

PART FOUR: The Past

Petra

Twenty-Five

When Petra shut the side gate of number fifty-three Princess Street her heart was racing. Tina was standing beside her, centimetres away, rubbing her hands together with the cold. Petra turned and faced the overgrown path round the side of the house. In the dark it seemed to go on a long way, like a tunnel. She walked on, trying not to show any hesitation. Something scuttled across the path in front and Tina reached out and grabbed her arm.

'It's just a mouse,' Petra said.

It had sounded bigger though – maybe a rat? She moved her feet about, hoping to scare it off.

'What you doing?' Tina said.

'Nothing.'

'This is horrible.'

'I know. We can't go back now though. Not after telling Mandy we were going in.'

In the daylight the garden had looked wild but vibrant. Now the bushes appeared to have merged into one solid shape that loomed up against them. It was silent too, the noises from the street cut off by the side gate. It felt like they were in the middle of a wood. Petra reached the corner of the building. Tina was close behind. The back garden spread out before them, deep and indistinct. The big trees that Petra remembered arced over the rest. Somewhere, in the middle of the garden, hung the old swing, but Petra couldn't make it out.

They went towards the back door, Tina sticking close to the wall.

'I've got to find the key,' Petra said.

She began to feel the wall to the right of the door. The ivy was thick and tightly wound. She tried to visualise the exact spot that she'd seen it the time they'd come into the garden. Her hand sunk into the bristly foliage, feeling an unpleasant sharpness. Seconds later she felt the hook. The key was there. She slipped it off and felt around for the lock. As quietly as she could she opened the back door of the house.

'Come on!' she whispered.

'I don't think I want to go in there. There might be a ghost,' Tina said.

Petra sighed. She turned and stood close to Tina, putting her mouth to her ear.

'There are no ghosts. You'll have to trust me about this but I know the old man who lives here is going to get robbed by someone. That's why I'm going in there: to *warn* him. There were never any ghosts.'

'Oh.'

'We can go in and come out in less than five minutes. Tell him to ring the police. He won't know who *we* are but it might stop him losing his money.'

And it might stop Dad committing a crime.

She took Tina's hand. They should go in there *now* before she completely lost her nerve. She stepped inside, pulling Tina a few steps along with her. They were standing in a kitchen. Her eyes got used to the dark and she could see that it was a big room with a large table in the middle. Around the side were cupboards and there was a sink by the window. The door into the rest of the house was half open and there was a faint sheen of light coming from further up the hallway. She looked round to see Tina's face frozen, her mouth in a straight line. She squeezed her hand and walked forward.

There was a sound, a *thump*. Low and muffled, as if someone had punched a cushion. She felt Tina's hand gripping hers. Then there was a bang like something dropping from a height.

She felt Tina twist and pull her hand away. Without a word she backed off until she was at the door to the garden. She paused for a moment and stared at Petra, her face screwed up with worry. She shook her head rapidly then turned away. A second later the doorway was empty and Tina was gone. Petra was on her own. She felt unstable, light-headed. She wanted to run after Tina but she'd come here to do something and it was important that she stayed. Maybe the noises she'd heard were made by the old man, dropping things.

Her legs felt weak but she walked forward and stepped into the hallway. Opposite were the stairs. To her left the living room door was partially open and threw a strip of light onto the hall floor. It was perfectly quiet. She tiptoed across the lit floor and into the dark stairwell by the front door. A hat stand was there, heavy with coats. There was a narrow space between it and the front door and she slipped into it. Now

215

she could see a sliver through the opening of the living room door but not much else. She glanced up the stairs. It was black. She would catch her breath and then go into the living room and face Mr Merchant.

There was a sudden movement from the living room. A set of footsteps seemed to go from one side to the other. Then there was the sound of a different set of footsteps.

Mr Merchant wasn't alone.

She stayed still and quiet, hardly drawing breath. A voice sounded.

'We just want what's owed! That's all. Why are you being so secretive? It's not even your money, old man. It belongs to someone else.'

A voice mumbled something but Petra couldn't quite catch the words. There were footsteps. There was definitely more than one person moving around. A figure came to the door. It opened fully and the light fell into the hall and stairwell. Her chest contracted. A man was standing with his back to her. She sunk in beside a coat and pulled the front of it across her body and face. It was thick with dust and smelt. She closed her eyes and heard the sound of talk.

'How long are we going to keep asking him? Constantine wants his money now! How long?'

There was a reply from somewhere else in the room. She opened her eyes and peeped out of the side of the coat. She knew the voice immediately. It was her dad. Fingers tightened inside her chest. She'd known he was involved but she hadn't wanted to actually *see* him there. If she could just slip away, get out. She was too late to do any good for Mr Merchant. The robbery would go ahead and she was stuck behind the coats. The first man turned round then, pulling his mobile out of his pocket and pressing buttons. The sight of him gave her a start. His face was covered with a balaclava. Only his eyes and mouth could be seen. It made her feel sick. It suddenly felt dangerous. He was listening to someone talking and saying, 'Yeah, I know. Yeah . . . I know . . .' Then he went back into the living room.

She saw Mr Merchant then. The old man was tied to a chair. There was a belt fastened around his chest and arms, and his legs were held with strips of cloth. He looked weak, his head lolling. He was wearing a shirt and tie as he had been on the day he waved to her through the window. The collar looked tight and his skin was puckered up around it. He appeared bewildered, as if he had no idea what was happening. Her dad was standing beside him. He was also wearing a balaclava but she'd have known him anywhere. The old man's face turned from her dad to the other man and back again.

Petra wanted to shout out but her throat was clamped tight.

The man on the phone said something and her dad seemed to sigh or shrug. Then he knelt down beside the old man and began to speak right into his ear. Petra couldn't hear his words but she saw that one of his hands was resting on the old man's chest as if he was about to pat him gently. Petra looked away. Something was in the air, something terrible. The front door was beside her. What if she opened it and ran out and cried out for help? She saw then that it was bolted at the top and bottom and she wouldn't be able to reach.

Her dad's voice got louder, angrier.

She could run along the hallway and out through the kitchen. There was too much light though. She would be seen and she might not even get very far. Her dad would rage at her. She looked back to the living room and she saw her dad's hand move closer to the throat of the old man. She felt faint, as if she might fold up on the spot. The other man spoke.

'Just tell us where it is! Just open your mouth and say the words. It's only money! And it's not yours! Otherwise he will hurt you! Why would you want him to do that?'

Mr Merchant's head seemed to slump. Her dad swore loudly. Then he took the sides of the chair and pushed it away from him. Petra watched in terror as the chair fell over, dragging Mr Merchant with it. It lay on its side on the floor, the old man still attached. He was facing away from her but she could see his head falling to the side. Her leg moved as if she would step out of her hiding place and go and help him, show her face so that her dad would stop.

She couldn't move though.

Her dad walked round the other side and she could see him pull a strip of material out of his pocket. He knelt down and tied it round Mr Merchant's mouth. Then he stood up and aimed a kick at the chair, making it skewer off. There was a gurgling sound coming from Mr Merchant but Petra couldn't watch any more. She crept out from the coats, stepped round the beam of light from the living room and up the stairs, taking them two at a time until she was three-quarters of the way up, out of sight. She sat down and huddled into the bannisters, her arms around her knees as she stared through the gaps. She heard banging and scraping. She pressed her thumbs against her eyelids because she didn't want to picture the chair being dragged around the room. There was shouting and thumping and she made herself as small as she could, shrinking into the corner of the stair. She was trembling with fright, her hands shaking in front of her face.

Then it stopped and there was silence.

A voice spoke. Petra didn't want to hear so she put her fingers in her ears, but it didn't block the sound out.

'Did you have to do that? Now we'll never find the money.'

'You said to make it real. To scare him.'

'I didn't tell you to kill him. He's no good to us dead.'

There was swearing. Her dad was mumbling, his words unclear as if he was far across the room.

'OK, let's trash the place. We might find it ourselves.'

'No, no . . . Let's get out . . .'

The other man appeared at the door and went down the hallway below where Petra was sitting. Her dad came to the door. He pulled his balaclava off and she saw his face. He looked hot and flustered, like someone she didn't know. He walked along the hall. She heard the footsteps go through the kitchen and then the back door slamming. When she was sure they'd gone she stood up and walked down the stairs. She went to the door of the living room. She gasped when she saw Mr Merchant lying under the upturned chair, his head at an odd angle, his face turned away from her.

This was her dad's work.

There was blood and she turned away from it, not wanting to look at him. She saw the room of an old sick man. Her eyes took in the single bed along the wall and beside it the oxygen tank, its feeds and mask still attached. Opposite the fireplace and television was the red velvet armchair that she'd heard Nathan Ball talking about. Behind it was wooden panelling that had been pulled away. She felt her head drop with shame. If she had come in earlier, this afternoon, when she first saw Nathan Ball hanging around, she could have told Mr Merchant. He would have rung the police and none of this would have happened. But she'd left it until it was too late.

There was a noise.

It was the sound of the back door opening. They were coming back.

She looked round the room in panic. She couldn't let them find her here. She stepped across to the red velvet chair and knelt down behind it. Footsteps came up the hallway, hurrying. Her dad came back into the room alone. He was mumbling under his breath. He went across to Mr Merchant's body and squatted down.

'You stupid old man,' he whispered.

Was he checking that he was really dead? Was he ashamed and going to try to help him in some way? She could see he was struggling with the belt that had been fastened around the old man's chest. It came free and he pulled it out inch by inch. Mr Merchant fell forward. Her dad stood up and began to thread the belt through the loops on his own jeans. She'd seen him do that at home. When she'd been ironing his shirt and he'd been getting reading to go out. 'How do I look?' he'd said. Now he did up the buckle and looked round. His eye paused on the place where she was hiding.

Had he seen her?

A moan escaped from her lips.

'Petra?' he said.

He stared at her in horror. She focused on his face. How could the sight of his daughter affect him more than the body of a dead old man? He seemed frozen. She stood up and walked around the edge of the room slowly. He came towards her, putting his hands out as if he wanted her to hold them.

'What are you doing here?' he said.

'You killed him.'

He shook his head and came closer to her. He glanced at the door and back as if he wanted to stop her going there. She stood still and put her two hands out. His face relaxed and he stepped towards her but she launched herself towards him and gave him a fierce push so that he stumbled backwards onto the floor.

Then she staggered out of the room.

Twenty-Six

Petra ran. She raced along Princess Street. She took breaths in great mouthfuls and turned into the next road and kept going. She didn't dare stop to see if her dad was coming after her. She passed by her school which was in darkness and slipped round the side of it to the path that she and Tina sometimes used to get to the park. There were lights dotted along it but she stepped into a recess and stood behind a tree. From where she was she could see the street beyond and she focused on it intently, expecting to see her dad passing, perhaps stopping, trying to find her.

But he didn't come. She waited for what seemed like a long time.

Then she stepped out of her hiding place and walked back to the street. Looking right and left, making sure he was nowhere to be seen, she began to walk. It had started to rain and she moved quicker, striding swiftly along as if she had to be somewhere. She left her school behind and headed towards Holloway Road. She continued walking, not sure of which direction she was heading. The street was busy with people coming home from work, getting off buses and struggling with umbrellas. The traffic was queueing, the lights of the cars illuminating the rain. As she passed each vehicle she could hear snatches of music or voices from the radio inside.

She was wet and cold. Her hands were trembling.

She stopped at a small van that sold drinks by the tube station. She bought a hot chocolate and then stood in the doorway of an empty shop and drank it slowly, feeling the burning liquid on her tongue and letting it lie there before swallowing. She didn't know what she was doing there. She had no idea where she was heading. She had no notion of what she was going to do. When she finished she walked out of the doorway and headed towards Angel. The shopping centre would be warm and would stay open until late. She could stay there while she worked out what to do.

What to do.

She faltered in her step. Her dad had just *killed a man*.

The memory made her stomach lurch and she thought, for a moment, that she was going to be sick. She steadied herself though and caused a couple of people to sidestep her, to make irate comments, to look back crossly at her for holding them up. But she could only think of Mr Merchant lying on the floor of his living room, partly tied to a chair. The image made something in her stomach claw at her. She remembered her dad unclasping the belt from around the old man's arms and chest and calmly threading it through his own trousers.

What about Nathan Ball? He hadn't been there but he'd been driving a white van around. Had he been waiting for a text to say that they'd found the money? Had he picked up her dad and the other man outside number fifty-three Princess

Street, expecting one of them to be holding a bag of cash? Instead they'd got into the van with murder on their hands.

She stopped and leant against a shop window. It was wet and the water soaked into her shoulder and arm. She didn't care. She preferred to be uncomfortable than to dwell on what had happened. She thought of Tina. At least she hadn't been there to see it. She'd run off frightened and was probably sitting at home right now or possibly she'd gone to Mandy's house and Mandy's mother was fussing over her. Then Tina would go back home where her own mum would be waiting. Her dad would be miles away in South London with his beautician, but at least he wouldn't have any blood on his hands.

Would *her* dad go round to Tina's to look for her?

She walked on. It was a long way to Angel but she kept going.

The shopping centre wasn't so busy. It had a weary air about it as though people were longing to get their purchases and just go home. She walked aimlessly around, pretending to look into shop windows, but really she wasn't focusing on anything. In her mind she was still seeing Mr Merchant tied to a chair in his bedsit living room. Her dad was there wearing a balaclava, trying to persuade the old man to tell them where the money was.

What was she going to do about it?

Go to the police?

She began to cry and found it difficult to catch her breath in her throat. A couple of people were looking her way. She had to get out of there. She needed to go somewhere where she could sit and think. She left the shopping centre and headed off into the dark streets. It took a while to get to Zofia's because she'd only ever walked there from Angel once before. The house was in darkness but Petra could see, through the front-door glass, a hint of light from the back of the hallway. She pressed the bell and felt the sound vibrate. Moments later the hall light came on and footsteps sounded. The door flew open and Zofia stood there, her face stern.

'My God, it's nearly ten. Your father has been here looking for you!'

Of course her dad would go to Zofia's house. He knew how close they were.

Zofia stepped forward and looked out into the street.

'And your friend? Where is she?' Zofia said. 'The police have been called to look for both of you.'

'The police?'

The police? Her dad had called the *police*? After what had happened? She began to shake her head. Zofia had her by the hand and pulled her into the house.

'I get you nice towel and get you warm, then I call your father.'

'No, no, no, *please*, Zofia. Don't call my dad. Please, I beg you, don't call him. I don't want him to know where I am.'

'You rowed with him?'

'No. It's worse than that. It's much worse . . . Please, Zofia, don't call him. Don't call anyone.'

'But your friend?'

'I don't know what you mean . . .'

'Come, see . . .'

Zofia pulled her by the hand into the kitchen. The small television on the side was on the twenty-four-hour news channel. Zofia manoeuvred Petra until she was sitting down.

'I'll get a towel,' she said. 'You watch the news.'

225

The newscaster was talking about a war in a Middle Eastern country but Petra was watching the rolling news across the bottom of the screen. The words 'Two twelve-year-old girls missing in North London' made her sit up. Zofia came back in with a large orange towel. She put it round Petra's shoulders.

'You see. Is on the news. Two girls go missing. You and friend. The pictures will come up in a minute.'

Just then the newsreader moved on.

'The whereabouts of two twelve-year-old friends in Holloway, North London, is giving cause for concern. The girls, Christine Pointer and Petra Armstrong, are friends and had been spending time together over the holidays. They were last seen about five thirty this evening by another girl outside a newsagent's on Princess Street. The police have sent out an alert and are actively searching for the girls.'

Two photographs filled the screen. They were the school photographs taken some weeks before. Headshots of Petra and Tina.

'I don't understand. Where is Tina?' Petra said.

Zofia was sitting on a chair beside her.

'Where have you been? I must ring your father.'

'No, no,' she said, 'I don't want to see him ever. Never . . .'

Petra turned and hugged Zofia. She buried her face into Zofia's neck, and gripped her arms tightly. She held onto Zofia, wishing she could stay like that for ever. Zofia patted her head and tried to pull away.

'Tell me what has happened. Tell me now. Start from beginning.'

Petra sat back and began to tell Zofia what had happened.

'You will sleep in my bed. I have a sleeping bag,' Zofia said.

It was past midnight. Petra had stopped crying a while ago. Zofia had listened to her story with dismay and shock and anger. They had turned the television off and Zofia had said they should go to bed and that they would work out what to do in the morning. The police had not been mentioned. Zofia's face had settled into a grave look. She was walking round in her slippers and looked tiny. Her bags were packed and stacked round the room, ready for her to go back to Poland. Petra looked at them and felt a sharp pain. Soon she would be gone.

'I won't be able to go to sleep,' Petra said.

Zofia reached into one of the boxes. She pulled out a DVD. It was series five of *Friends*: the one where Monica and Chandler get together and try to keep it a secret from the others.

'We'll watch some,' she said.

Zofia slipped the disc into the player, picked her sleeping bag up off the floor and laid it on the top of the bed alongside Petra. She kicked her slippers off and sat on top. Petra felt her close, her perfume heavy. She glanced at the screen, at Chandler and Monica, and then back to Zofia whose face sagged with worry

After a while of watching the programme Petra drifted off to sleep.

Twenty-Seven

When Petra woke it was light; past nine o'clock.

Zofia was not in the room and her sleeping bag had been moved from the bed. Petra sat up quickly and looked around. Even though she'd slept for a long time, her head felt heavy, her eyes still swollen from the crying she'd done. The memory of the previous night came back to her like a door opening onto a cold place. She felt a quickening at her throat and threw the duvet back, looking for her clothes. She remembered the long talk she and Zofia had had the night before. Zofia had been upset at first but became calm as time went on. As they lay on the bed watching *Friends*, the noise of the front door opening and shutting had sounded and Zofia had said, 'It's OK, some people having a late night.'

Even though the people who lived in Zofia's house changed from week to week, Zofia knew them all. 'He plays music at two in the morning. She leaves dishes in sink. She never learnt to wash out bath when finished!' But Zofia seemed friendly enough with them. Would any of them know who Petra was? Would they watch the news and say, 'I recognise that girl'?

She'd worried about this for a while but then drifted in and out of sleep. Each time she opened her eyes Zofia seemed to be awake. She'd been sitting bolt upright on the bed beside her, staring into the dark. Hours later she'd seen her standing over by the window holding one of the curtains to the side and looking out. Early in the morning when it was still dark and the clock showed 5.59, Zofia was sitting on the side of the bed, her elbows on her knees and her head in her hands. Each time Petra had wanted to say something, to reach out and comfort her, but she felt the pull of sleep, her eyes like weights, her limbs slumping, her thoughts tumbling into darkness.

Now she pulled on her clothes and was doing up her trainers when Zofia walked in. She was carrying a mug of tea and a plate of toast and jam. She smiled when she saw Petra and placed the hot things on the bedside cabinet.

'You have a drink and you eat and then later we talk about what to do.'

Zofia was dressed and looked strange. She had on black trousers and a white blouse. She was wearing her usual heels and her hair was pulled up in a sombre back clip. Petra looked at her hand as she gave her the mug of tea. Her nails were plain and short. Had they been like that last night? She couldn't remember. This was a different Zofia. She looked serious, stern even, as though she might be on the brink of giving Petra a telling off.

'I have to go and see my friend with van who is taking me to Poland. I have to give him money by today. He lives a few streets away. When I come back we will talk and decide what we can do. You eat, drink. You can have a shower. Just don't let anyone in the house see you. OK?'

Petra nodded. Zofia stood by the door, looking as though there was something else she wanted to say.

'I will see you soon,' she said.

She closed the door quietly behind her.

Petra didn't like being alone there. She went over to the window that looked out onto the street. She saw Zofia walking along, pulling her coat tightly round her.

She put the television on and turned to the news channel. The mug of tea and plate of toast sat untouched as she watched. The story had changed. The police had gone into number fifty-three Princess Street and found Mr Merchant's body. Mandy must have told them that they'd gone into the house. The words 'Breaking news' were flashing and the details were scrolling past. 'Sources suggest that the two missing girls, Christine Pointer and Petra Armstrong, had entered the house of George Merchant, a retired accountant. On gaining access to this property police found the body of an elderly man thought to be Mr Merchant. There was no sign of the two girls. A news conference is due shortly, where the parents of the girls will make an appeal to the public.'

Petra sat stiffly, her back straight, her neck rigid. There were other items of news but after a few moments the press conference came on. There was a table covered in microphones. A lot of background noise could be heard and then a police officer sat down in one of the chairs. The camera pulled away to show three people taking seats. Petra saw Alison, Tina's mum, and beside her was Bobby, Tina's dad. Then she saw her dad, sitting behind one of the microphones, smoothing his hair down. She looked intently at the screen, ignoring the comments of the police officer who was talking to the press. She focused on him. He was wearing a shirt and tie and a jacket. He looked smart. She wondered if he'd ironed it himself that morning. She could see he was uneasy because his gaze kept shifting around the room and he was fiddling with his tie. Alison and Bobby Pointer were leaning in towards each other.

Alison spoke to the camera.

'Tina and Petra? We want you both to know we don't think you've done anything wrong. If you ran away or went somewhere that you weren't allowed to go we won't be angry with you. We just want you to come home. We love you and we want to see you.'

Her dad had taken a piece of paper out of his inside jacket pocket. He unfolded it as flashlights went off. Then he read.

'Petra and Tina, we are worried about you both. Please come home. If you can't come home please get in touch with us so that we know you are safe. Or if anyone has seen our girls please get in touch with the police –'

Alison broke in.

'Tina, we won't be mad at you. You are not in trouble. Just come home please.'

She was crying and Bobby was comforting her. Petra's dad was looking round at them and Petra couldn't see his face. Then he turned back to the camera. He had a grim expression and his jaw was twitching with tension. He looked up at one of the cameras and she seemed to catch his eye for a moment.

You killed a man, she thought. *I know that you didn't care and you did it for the money.*

Petra turned the television off. She looked at the bedside clock. It was almost ten. She wondered how long Zofia would be. She was going to see the man with the van about the trip to Poland. She was due to go in two days. Could Petra get her to change her mind and stay? Maybe then she could go to the police and tell them what she'd seen. If her dad was arrested then she could stay with Zofia. But even as she thought this she knew it wouldn't happen. She wouldn't be allowed to stay with Zofia. She would be picked up by Pam Fellows and taken to some nice foster family miles away. There would be a new school, the attempt to make new friends. And all the while everyone would know that her dad was a murderer.

And where was Tina? *Where* was Tina?

Could she even tell the police? As much as she was revolted by what her dad did, could she see him sent to prison for many years, even if it was what he deserved? Could she be responsible for that?

She thought of Mr Merchant lying on the floor of his room, dead. It made her squirm and pull her knees up so that she was sitting in a ball. At least Tina hadn't seen her dad do such a thing. She remembered the two of them rehearsing for The Red Roses: standing side by side in front of a long mirror, like sisters. Blood sisters. Poor Tina had been frightened and run out of the house. Could it be, in those moments, on the street, someone had picked her up in a car? Someone she knew? A stranger? Was she trapped in someone's house at that very minute? At the same time as the appeals were going on, the house-to-house searches, was Tina stuck in a room wondering what was happening to her?

Petra was crying again.

Where was Zofia? She uncurled herself and walked across to the window. A police car drove past. Seeing it made her stand back sharply, as if she might be seen from there and recognised. But it was just a squad car patrolling the streets. It wasn't there for her.

When was Zofia coming back?

She sat down on the bed. Zofia had been shocked at what she'd told her but she'd had an expression on her face as if to say, *I knew it would happen!* As if she alone understood what her dad was capable of. He'd hurt her a couple of weeks before and maybe even before that too. Possibly Zofia would like to see him in prison. Perhaps that's where she'd gone now, to the police. She might at this very moment be informing them about what had happened and in a moment that very same squad car that she'd just seen would double back and park outside the house and two officers would come for her.

She couldn't help what Zofia was going to do or not but she couldn't get picked up by the police. She didn't know if she could stand and point her finger at her own dad even though she was appalled by him. If the police came then it was important that she should *not* be there.

She grabbed her jacket and put it on. She opened the door slightly to make sure that no one else in the house was around. She went out onto the landing and then swiftly down the stairs. She opened the front door and walked out into the street. She pulled her coat tight and had her collar up, tucking her hair away to try to look different from the school photo that was on the television. She started walking away from Zofia's house when she heard someone call.

'Wait, wait . . .'

She looked round and saw Zofia coming up the street. She had a carrier bag over one arm. There was no one with her. She seemed to break into a trot and rushed up to Petra. She grabbed both her arms and looked at her with concern. The carrier bag swung to and fro. Petra felt guilty. She was becoming a huge burden on her. She didn't want that. The one person she didn't want to hurt was Zofia.

'Where are you going?'

'I thought . . . I thought you might go to the police . . .'

Zofia shook her head.

'But you are going back to Poland.'

Zofia nodded.

'I don't know what to do,' Petra said hopelessly.

'Come inside. Let's talk.'

Petra sat on the bed but Zofia stayed standing. She kept her coat on and it looked as though she was going to make a speech. Petra wished she'd sit down beside her, link her arm or hold her hand.

'This is what I think you should do,' Zofia said. 'You should go to police. Tell them everything. Talk to the social lady. She will find you a good family. You live with them until you are eighteen.'

Petra shook her head furiously.

'I can't tell the police about my dad! I just can't!'

'After you are eighteen you could come and see me in Poland.'

'No, no . . .'

'This is difficult situation.'

Just then the front door sounded. It closed with a bang which meant someone from one of the other rooms had probably gone out.

'And we have this problem that someone will see you and know who you are.'

'I could live with you,' Petra whispered.

Zofia shook her head. 'I could go to prison for this. Police are looking for you.'

'You care about me. I know you do. I care about you.'

'I don't know. I don't. I have to think . . .'

She finally sat down on the bed beside her. Petra took her hand. It was hot, fiery. She traced the line of her nails and leant her head against Zofia's shoulder. Zofia reached down to pick up the carrier bag. She pulled out a box of black hair dye. Petra looked at it.

'We need to make you look different.'

'OK. I'll use this.'

'Not just this. We need to cut . . .'

Zofia got up and went across to her suitcase. She undid the zip a few centimetres and pulled out a large cosmetics bag. She took out a pair of scissors and walked towards the bed. Petra didn't care about her hair. She just wanted to stay with Zofia.

Twenty-Eight

On Friday, just after seven, Petra put on the new coat that Zofia had gone out and bought for her that day. She looked at herself in the mirror. She had short black hair and looked very different: a bit younger perhaps and stern. They were getting ready to go out. Zofia had given her instructions. 'I leave the house first. You follow me one minute later. We walk separately. Marya's flat only five minutes away.'

Zofia made sure no one was about when she slipped downstairs. She went out of the front door and then Petra counted to sixty and followed her. She could see her further up the street. She walked with her head down and wondered why they were going to Marya's. Zofia said she had to pick up some things to take to Poland but Petra didn't think this would be uppermost in Zofia's mind right now. Since their talk earlier in the day, since the hair makeover, they'd not said anything about the situation. Zofia had gone out shopping then continued packing up her stuff: four suitcases and two holdalls. Petra had watched her with apprehension. Every jumper or pair of socks she packed, every pair of spikey heels she forced down the side of the suitcase, seemed ominous.

Soon she would be gone and Petra would be on her own. She wanted to say something to raise the subject again but Zofia was preoccupied, her chin pointed down to the ground, her nails unadorned, her hands busy.

They'd watched the news and saw that the police were in and out of the house on Princess Street. It looked as though the area had been cordoned off. Petra watched the comings and goings with great trepidation. All the time she kept thinking about Tina. Where had she gone when she ran out into the dark?

Petra thought of Nathan Ball in his van. Could Tina have run out of the side gate at just the moment that Nathan Ball's van returned to the street? Had he seen her come out of the house and out of the garden? He would have realised that she'd been in the house when her dad and the other man was there. Could he have stopped her, spoken to her, perhaps pretended that he was related to Mr Merchant in some way and told her she had go with him?

Had Nathan Ball taken Tina away somewhere?

It couldn't be. Her dad would know. Nathan Ball would have rung him, texted him, turned up on the balcony and told him. Whatever bad things her dad had done he wouldn't let anything happen to Tina. Would he? He liked Tina, he'd always play his ringtones for her and when he had money he often gave Petra a fiver to give to Tina so that she could 'get herself something nice'. But Nathan Ball had no link to Tina. Could he have panicked and thought that Tina had seen too much? Maybe he did something to her to keep her quiet. Petra pictured him slipping out of the driver's seat into the dark street and walking along behind Tina, maybe slipping his hand over her mouth and pulling her backwards to the van.

Petra faltered. She couldn't carry on. Her life seemed to have spun off into some dark and cruel place where people did things that she couldn't understand. Up ahead Zofia paused as if she sensed that Petra had stopped. She turned and came back to her, taking her hand firmly and pulling her forward. Petra walked tentatively as if she were on a kind of rickety bridge and every step might bring the whole thing crashing down.

At Marya's old flat Petra waited on the street while Zofia used a key to open the front door. She went in and beckoned Petra to follow her.

Zofia had a phone in her hand and Petra noticed that it wasn't her usual mobile. It looked like a basic pay as you go.

'You got a new phone?'

'I need to contact someone and don't want any records.'

Zofia was stiff and brusque. She was nervous. It made Petra feel apprehensive. She followed her through the flat. It was sparingly furnished but there were signs that someone had been there until recently: a couple of carrier bags had collected in the corner of the hall and on the table in the kitchen a box of tissues sat next to a half full bottle of Pepsi. The fridge door was held open by a chair and on the windowsill was a vase of flowers that were still in bloom.

Zofia stood awkwardly at the table. There was a door behind her that led to another room. Petra glimpsed a washing machine through it.

'What have we come for? Are we picking something up?' Petra said.

Zofia exhaled loudly.

'Your father is coming here,' she said.

Petra was shocked. She looked around as though he might already be there.

'To take me home?'

'No, no. No.'

She wasn't ready to *see* her dad. She didn't think she ever wanted to see him again. Zofia put her hand on Petra's arm.

'I have to talk to him. I have to put things straight with him. Otherwise I don't know what to do about you. I just don't know.'

'I can't see him!' Petra said. 'What if he brings the police with him? I can't see the police. I just can't.'

'He won't. He doesn't like police. He'll be on his own. That's what I told him. He won't even know you are here. But I want *you* to hear what he says.'

There was a knock on the front door. Zofia looked towards the sound and nodded.

'Is on time. You go into utility room. Shut the door and keep the light off. Just stay there and hear what he says.'

'I don't want to be here if he's here,' Petra said, chewing her lip.

'You have to hear his words. Otherwise you and me cannot be together. You have to trust me.'

Petra stared at Zofia. Tonight she looked frightened, her face pale. She pushed at Petra's arm with surprising force.

'Go.'

Petra went into the utility room. It was small, with only enough room for a washing machine and a tumble dryer. An empty clothes horse stood folded up alongside. She shut the door. There was no window so the room was dark, like a black cubicle. She sat down, her back to the door. She couldn't hear any sound from the kitchen, only a mumble of voices further away. She wondered why Zofia had asked her dad to come here and not to her own house. Maybe she was fearful of the police following him and stumbling on Petra before she'd decided what to do. Or possibly there were just too many other people around at Zofia's.

What *would* she do? Would she keep Petra with her? What was the point of talking to her dad?

She heard her dad's voice first.

'This better be important, Soph. I'm pretty preoccupied at the moment.'

There was the sound of chairs being pulled out and sat on. Her dad's voice had a sneer in it. Petra recognised it from times when he was being sarcastic.

'What can I do for you?'

She pictured him leaning back in the chair, his arms crossed.

A ringtone sounded. Petra thought it was Zofia's new mobile. It had a funny old-fashioned sound like bells tinkling.

'Excuse me, Jason.'

Zofia was answering it.

'Henryk. I am in the flat now. You are outside? Good. Jason is here too.'

'What's going on?' Her dad's voice was faintly high, disbelieving.

'My friend, Henryk, is outside. He is waiting for me. He has key. In fifteen minutes he will come in to check that I am all right.'

'Soph . . . What's going on?'

Petra was puzzled. What was Zofia doing? Who was Henryk?

'If you hit me he will know. He is big as you, Jason, and he has weapon. He used to be in the army. He will hurt you.'

'What's this drama all for, Soph? My daughter is missing, in case you didn't know. I've got more important stuff to deal with than your stupid . . .'

It sounded as though the chair was moving, as if her dad was getting ready to leave.

'I know where Petra is,' Zofia said.

'What?'

'She is safe. I want to talk to you about her.'

'She went to you! I knew she would. I came round to you last night. I asked you. You lied to me . . .'

The chair legs creaked as if her dad had shifted. Perhaps he'd leant forward across the table.

'No, no, Jason. She came much later. Very late. She was in a state and I know that you know why so please no bully stuff with me. She did not want to see you. She begged me not to contact you or the police.'

'Where is she?'

'She is safe.'

'What about her friend?'

'She's not with her friend. She doesn't know where friend is.'

Dad doesn't know what happened to Tina. This was important to Petra.

241

'I want to see Petra.'

'She doesn't want to see you.'

'She's a kid. She's twelve. She doesn't get to make those kinds of decisions.'

'She's bright. She knows the difference between right and wrong and she knows that you killed accountant.'

There was a moment's silence. Petra tried to picture her dad's face. When he spoke again his voice was different.

'She thought she saw something . . . She misinterpreted . . . She . . .'

'Jason, she knows. She was frightened to death when she came to me. She knows her own father kill accountant. Don't try to deny it. I believe her. I know what you are like and you talked about accountant for many weeks. I believe it.'

'Soph . . . It was an accident. We didn't go there with that intention. It got out of hand. It was a job I had to do for someone else. They were threatening me. The old man owed them money. I could have got hurt if I hadn't done it. The old man just would not say where the money was. Things got rough.'

His voice was low, just above a whisper. Petra felt her jaw clamping together as she remembered the scene in the house on Princess Street: an old man who was tied and belted to a chair then beaten. Although she hadn't been able to bear watching the blows she'd heard each of them and then she'd seen him lying twisted on the floor with blood on his shirt collar.

'It was this other guy. Nathan put me on to him. He was out of control.'

It wasn't true. Petra felt her head hanging as if in shame. It was her dad who'd started the attack.

'No matter,' Zofia said, 'is in the past. Petra does not want to come back to you. She does not want to live with you any more.'

'She can't say that. She's my daughter.'

'If you insist that she comes back then she will tell police what she saw.'

'She won't tell anyone. I'm her dad. It was an accident. I'll explain it to her. There's no point in me going to prison for something I didn't mean to do!'

Not true. Not true. Petra hugged her knees.

'She might not tell, Jason, but I will. If you make her come back I will go police. I will tell them what she told me. I know names. Mr Constantine. Nathan Ball . . .'

'Why? What's it to you? What's any of it got to do with you?'

His voice had risen and he had moved position, Petra was sure. Maybe he was leaning across the table and speaking right into Zofia's face. Maybe his finger was raised up, pointing at her. She'd seen him do that before.

'I care for Petra,' Zofia said, her voice coming from exactly the same place. 'I don't like the life she has with you. Before, when we finish, I have no choice. She is your daughter and there is nothing I can do. But now that you have done this thing you give up right to her.'

'What?'

Her dad sounded incredulous.

'You bitch . . . You can't tell me what to do . . .'

The chair's legs scraped along the floor and Petra's shoulder blades tensed. Was he going to hit Zofia? If he did Petra would not be able to stay where she was. She would face him. She would not let Zofia get hurt again.

'Jason, Petra knows I am seeing you. If you hit me she will go to police and I will go with her. You will have to kill me if you want me to shut up. And Henryk is outside. He will come in soon. He will hurt you. You should believe me when I say I will not leave Petra with you. You give her a sad poor life. It took me a while to really see it and now I can do something about it. Sit down . . . We talk . . . You get away with dead accountant and I take Petra to Poland with me. She starts a new life. We say nothing to police.'

Petra listened intently. She wished she could see what was going on. Her dad was probably staring darkly at Zofia and maybe she was keeping eye contact, not prepared to back down. A bargain was being made. Her dad's freedom for Petra to be with Zofia. Was it right? What about Mr Merchant? Did he not deserve some sort of justice? But if Petra gave her information up she wouldn't be able to be with Zofia, she would live in foster care, and one day her dad would come out of prison and she would have to see him again.

'Why did you even tell me this? Why didn't you just take her?'

'Because one day other girl will turn up. Maybe alive. Maybe not. Then you would wonder what happen to your daughter and you would think of me. I do not want to see you coming after us in Poland.'

'You've thought this all out.'

'I have.'

'And Petra wants it?'

'She's afraid of you, Jason. Let her go.'

Petra heard the sound of a chair moving.

'What makes you think I won't still come after you?'

'Because wherever I am she will be there and I don't think you want to give her more pain.'

She could hear breathing. Her dad went to say something but stopped. There was a sound from the hallway. The front door opened and closed again. Heavy footsteps came up the hall.

'Is this your muscle boy?' her dad said.

'This is Henryk.'

'Your new boyfriend?'

'You should go, Jason. We don't need you.'

Petra flinched. Had Zofia meant to say *we*?

'She's here, isn't she?' her dad said.

Petra froze. She stood up stiffly and looked around the small space. There was no way out. If he wanted to see her he just had to push the door in.

'She doesn't want to see you. Just go, Jason.'

'Get out, Jason.' A deep male voice. A Polish voice.

There was a long silence. Petra wondered if her dad was squaring up to Henryk. Or was he looking round the room searching for her? It wouldn't take a second to work out where she had hidden. Then there were footsteps. For a moment Petra didn't know whether they were coming towards her or going away. She closed her eyes as she had done the previous night in Mr Merchant's hallway. If she kept them tightly shut she wouldn't have to see anything.

But the footsteps were walking away and then the front door slammed loudly. The utility room door opened and light flooded in.

'You heard everything?'

Petra nodded. Zofia stepped across and Petra hugged her. Petra could feel her going limp in her arms. She was clammy, her thin arms hanging. Then she seemed to stiffen up and stepped back. Behind her was a man Petra had never seen. He was wearing a khaki jacket and had a football scarf around his neck. He gave her a gruff nod and then walked out of the room.

'You happy with arrangement?'

'Yes.'

'Now we go.'

Zofia locked up the flat. Henryk was walking ahead. Petra looked up and down the street. There was no sign of her dad or his cab. Had she thought there might be? That he would wait for her and remonstrate?

When they got back to the house Zofia said, 'Now we will go. We bring bags down.'

'Tonight? I thought you were going on Sunday.'

'No, now. Henryk is here. We take the overnight ferry from Harwich. We drive through Holland. By morning we will be in Germany.'

They'd already taken the bags and cases downstairs and stacked them in the hallway. Henryk nodded at Zofia and packed the things into the van.

When they were finished, Zofia introduced him.

'This is Henryk Palka. He is an old friend. I know him from school but then he moved to Krakow and I didn't see him again until I came to London. He is taking us to Poland.'

Henryk stared at Zofia. His face broke into a smile. Then he looked at Petra.

'Henryk, this is my sister Klara. She's all grown up now.'

Henryk nodded. 'Luggage all finished?'

'He likes to talk in English. Is learning.'

'We are ready?' Henryk said.

They got into the van and drove north, out of the city, into the countryside, heading for Harwich.

PART FIVE: The Present

Mandy

Twenty-Nine

Mandy was standing outside number fifty-three Princess Street.

There was nothing left of the house or the garden, just two giant trees in the back corner. The debris left behind by the demolition company had been removed and the area was level. It looked neat and tidy. The fence was repaired and there were some men in suits on the site wearing yellow hats.

Debbie Howard, the counsellor, was standing beside her. Debbie had spent some time at Mandy's house. Their sessions were over and Mandy's mum had insisted that Debbie come for tea and cakes. Debbie had finished her research at the surgery and was returning to university. Mandy was walking her to the Tube station. It seemed only right to walk past the site of the old house.

'It's big. The house must have been large.'

'It was.'

'And your friends were drawn to it. I read some of the articles on the net.'

'They called them the Moth Girls. It doesn't quite explain it. Petra was the one who was fascinated by it. Tina just went along.'

'I wish I'd seen it when it was standing because we've spoken

251

about this house a lot. But *your* problems were to do with your friends. Not what happened to them here.'

'I think I understand that now. It makes me seem so shallow though.'

'The friendship thing was what loomed large in your life. When they disappeared everything was unresolved. Perhaps if their bodies had been found, if there had been a funeral, then you could have moved on. But, you know, Mandy, you seem so much better these last few times that we've spoken. You've talked so much less about Petra and that's good.'

'I've been feeling better.'

Debbie thought that she had cured Mandy. She didn't know that Mandy had other worries that had nothing to do with her friendship with Tina and Petra. Mandy held Petra's secret and in the weeks that had passed since their talk this knowledge had weighed heavily on her. She should go to the authorities. She knew this and yet she hadn't done it.

'Shall we walk on?' Debbie said, turning away from the site.

'Sure.'

Just then the door of the next house opened. Mandy looked round and saw a man emerging from it. He was big, overweight. He was wearing heavy glasses and his face was red. He moved slowly, locking the front door with a second key. Then he came along the path and out of the front gate. It was the man who'd shouted at her, Petra and Tina when they'd gone into the garden that day all those years ago. And Mandy had seen him in the supermarket a few days later. The angry neighbour. She hadn't set eyes on him since then but of course he still lived there. He took a minute to shut his gate and then turned round. She caught his eye and he stopped and looked puzzled. She felt she ought to say something but that was stupid because he didn't know her except from that one time.

'Mandy, I need to get a move on.'

'OK,' Mandy said and walked on with her.

At the Tube station Debbie gave Mandy a hug. It was a bit awkward but Mandy did her best to reciprocate. Across the road she noticed a police car pull up just after the lights. A police officer got out of the car. Several people looked round at it.

'I like your earrings,' Debbie said.

'I made them. Well, a girl at my school helped. Her mum makes this kind of stuff.'

'You've got my email and mobile number. Keep in touch. I'd like to know how you get on.'

'I will.'

Mandy watched her walk off. She was all in black as usual. Her handbag swung wildly as she walked, hitting her hip. When she got to the barriers she flipped it open, pulled out her Oyster card and placed it on the machine. Moments later she was gone. Mandy felt mildly relieved. The sessions with her had become difficult because she'd been holding back. It was hard talking about Petra and Tina when she had this *knowledge* weighing her down.

It hadn't all been bad though. They had started to talk about different things. Tommy Eliot for instance. 'Do you think your reliance on Tommy might stem from the same emotions that made you want Petra's approval?' Mandy had known she was right. She was too needy and she had admitted it. 'Oh,' Debbie had said, 'that old word "needy". It's often spoken about in such a negative way. And yet wasn't that why mankind survived when other species didn't? Isn't "need" one of the most important things that humans use to get on and to flourish? Don't look at it as a weakness. You need people. So what? Embrace it.'

So what if she needed people?

Mandy felt one of the earrings hanging through her hair. She'd used her own beads but Lucy's mum had shown her how to shape the wire using round-nosed pliers. They'd made four pairs that day and Mandy had enjoyed wearing them. Tommy had said, 'Fab earrings,' and she'd been pleased without feeling the old hurt that used to tinge any remark he made to her. She'd decided to make earrings for Christmas presents.

She shook her head. *Christmas*. How could she think of it when she was carrying this *thing* round with her? It was getting dark as she walked away from the Tube and along the shopfronts. Christmas decorations flashed on and off, even though there was more than a month to go. She made herself focus, not that it was ever far from her mind.

For a few days after seeing Petra she had agonised over whether to tell someone. Not because she wanted to give Petra's secret away but because she wondered if the knowledge that the fate of the two girls had been different might help the police find out what had really happened to Tina. Alison Pointer was always on her mind. Alison, who suffered every day because Tina was lost. Would it make her happy to know what had happened to her? Even if the news was bad?

Five years had gone by though. If she told the police about seeing Petra, how would it help? And would they even believe her if she told them? Might they not think that she'd conjured the whole thing up? She'd had sightings of Petra on the bus years before; might her 'sighting' of Petra now be construed as more of the same?

She noticed the policeman again, walking along the other side of the road. Then she recognised him. It was Officer Farraday. The man she'd seen weeks before when the house was being demolished. Now he'd appeared before her just as she'd been debating whether or not to tell Petra's story. Maybe it was a kind of sign. He stopped for a moment and talked to a boy on a bike, then he walked on. He saw her looking at him and seemed puzzled, but then he recognised her and raised his arm in a wave. He looked up and down at the traffic then crossed the road. As he sidestepped cars she thought, *It's too soon. I can't say anything; it's too soon.*

'Hello, Mandy.'

'Hi,' she said. 'How are you?'

'I'm well. And you?'

'I'm good.'

'Last time I saw you, at the house, you seemed a bit tense.'

'Well, it was quite a day.'

He nodded. 'I thought about you from time to time, especially when Alison Pointer came back from France.'

'Are you going off-duty?'

'No, I'm in the middle of a shift. I was going to get a sandwich and tea in the café. Do you want to join me? I've only got about fifteen minutes but I thought I'd take a break.'

'Sure.'

She went with him into a tiny café a couple of doors along from the Tube station. He got his food and she bought a can of drink. They sat at a window table on high stools facing the street and passers-by. They would only have a short time so Mandy decided to be brave and ask some questions.

'I wanted to ask you something about the case,' Mandy said.

'Fire away,' he said.

He was struggling to get the sandwich packet open. When he did he exhaled and took a giant bite.

'When the police were investigating, at the beginning, did they ever consider that the fate of the two girls could have been separate? In other words, something happened to Petra and something different happened to Tina?'

'Why? Have you remembered something?'

'No, no. I've just been thinking a lot about it.'

He sighed. 'The detectives pursued every possible scenario they could think of. Mostly they looked at the two girls disappearing together. They tried to link it to the murder of George Merchant, so they focused on gang crime, organised drugs crime. They even went down the paedophile road. Checked George Merchant's background, private life, old computers they found in his house. Nothing on any count. You name it they went with it.'

The street lights had come on outside. Instantly it looked darker than it had before; even the Christmas lights seemed sharper, more dramatic. Mandy was reminded of the painting she had looked at in Dr Shukla's surgery: *Automat*. It was a word for a self-service café, one that had vending machines, although they couldn't be seen in the picture. Only the girl was visible, sitting at a table, in what looked like the middle of the night. The picture had a sense of loneliness, as if the girl had nothing or nobody in the world, as if she was running away. Mandy thought of Petra. She had run away and she'd found a kind of happiness. Was it right that Mandy should spoil that? If she went to the police with her story then the newspapers would make it their job to find Petra, wherever she was. Did Mandy have the right to do that?

'Was it definite that whatever *happened* happened in that house?'

'Well, the forensics seemed to suggest it. Hairs were found in the living room that belonged to Petra and fibres were found on the kitchen door that matched a top which belonged to Alison Pointer. Tina borrowed it, you see. So it seems that they went in there and just never came out.'

Mandy felt stricken. Fibres from Tina's hoodie were found on the kitchen door. Not further into the property. This backed up Petra's story.

'Is the case closed?'

Officer Farraday shook his head, putting the last piece of sandwich in his mouth. He chewed for a minute. Then he pulled out a large handkerchief from his pocket and wiped his mouth, dabbing the corners.

'It will never be closed. Not unless they're found. There will always be a file open for those two girls. It's reviewed every year. Indeed this year, because of the demolition of the house, several people were interviewed again: neighbours, people who'd been in the street and seen the white van, the people who'd used the newsagent's. The detectives want to see if the activity around the demolition has jogged any memories.'

'It's hard to believe that no one saw anything.'

'You were the last person to see them, Mandy.'

'Why wasn't I interviewed recently?'

'A decision was made that your statement was complete and we could see no reason to dredge this all up in your life again. Although it seems as though you've been thinking about it a lot. In fact . . .'

He opened one of the flaps on his belt and pulled out a wad of small cards. He gave one to her. On it was his name, a mobile phone number and an email address.

'This is just in case something occurs to you. Even after all this time. You don't have to go to the station or anything dramatic like that. If you ring me and I don't answer, leave a message and I will get back to you as soon as I'm free.'

'Thanks,' she said and took the card.

After he left she sat in the café and stared out into the street.

She tried to think back to that night. It had been dark and the weather was cold. After Petra and Tina went through the side gate she'd walked away. She'd paused at the newsagent's but then was so cross that she'd just gone home. Why should she have waited around for them when they'd just left her there? Ten minutes later she'd been in her living room watching television, staring angrily at the screen. She must have missed Tina by a minute or so. If she'd just waited there, in the light from the newsagent's, she would have seen her emerge from the garden and they could have chatted and waited for Petra. Possibly Tina might have been critical of Petra. 'She's so obstinate!' she might have said and Mandy would have enjoyed that. But she'd gone home and when Tina came out of the side gate into the street there had been no one there.

Where had she gone?

Had she walked across to the newsagent's thinking that Mandy might be there? She thought then of Mr Johnson, the newsagent who always made a fuss of Tina when she went into the shop. That day when they were browsing the magazines for ideas for posters he came out from the behind the counter and stood closely to Tina, asking her if she'd like a magazine free of charge.

'No thank you, Mr Johnson,' she'd said.

'Call me Alfie,' he'd said and Mandy could hardly keep from bursting into giggles.

Had Tina gone into the newsagent's upset? Had Mr Johnson tried to comfort her? Was he a man who liked young girls? Mandy rested her head on her hands. Sometimes the world seemed full of shadowy people. You thought of them in one way but then they turned out to be something different. But Mr Johnson wasn't like that! He was friendly, nice. He was *old*: forty or more. Wouldn't he have just rung Tina's mum if she'd asked him to?

She got off the high stool and walked out of the café. The Christmas lights flashed on and off along the street. It had started to rain so she put her collar up and walked swiftly on. Officer Farraday's card sat heavy in her pocket. She didn't know what she was going to do. There was Alison Pointer to think about. And Petra.

She came into Princess Street and saw a car double-parked outside the site of the old house. It made her slow down and brought back the morning that she went onto the site when Petra stepped out of a car and stood looking through the fence.

This car had its hazard lights flashing on and off. When she got closer she saw that it was a minicab and a man had just got out of it and was paying the driver. He stepped onto the pavement just as she walked along. She paused to let him pass. He stopped and looked at her.

'I'm sorry, my dear, do I know you?'

'I don't think so,' she said, not wanting to explain.

His lips moved as if he might say something else but instead he nodded and headed for the gate of the house next door to the building site.

It was the next-door neighbour who had shouted them out of the garden.

She hadn't seen him for five years and that day she'd seen him twice.

Thirty

On Monday Mandy couldn't go to school. She wasn't ill but she stayed in bed and tried to read. She went on Facebook and then sorted out her beads and looked on the internet at the prices of the tools that Lucy's mother had to see if she could afford to buy them. She hopped from one thing to another. The whole weekend had been like that, not really settling down to anything.

She had some lunch and then found herself wandering out into the garden.

She went all the way down the back and to the bottom. It was cold, the sky gunmetal grey. The wind was irritable, rushing this way and that, making her hair fly across her face. She'd put her fleece on but still felt the chill of the air. There was a small shed there that was hardly ever used. Inside was an old kitchen table and chairs that her mum and dad had replaced. Instead of getting rid of them they'd put it there just in case someone in the family wanted it, but no one did. Mandy looked through the cloudy glass window and saw them stacked away, the chairs upended on the table the way they sometimes did in school so that the cleaner could sweep underneath. The place was draped with cobwebs. Like the house on Princess Street. Petra had described it as if she'd been in there but it had only been her father's words. She had told them about the ghosts as if she herself had experienced it. Tina had believed her completely, her eyes wide open, her face a mixture of wonder and fear. Mandy had never believed it. People lived in old houses all the time. Her house was old. People had lived and died here. There were no ghosts.

She turned her back to the shed and looked up the garden towards her house. Just then she heard the sound of the neighbour's back door opening. The fence was too high to see over so she didn't feel she had to say hello. She was glad. How would she explain why she was standing out in her garden on a cold November afternoon?

She was trying to jog her memory. She was trying to recall the one time that she'd been in the garden of the house on Princess Street. That garden no longer existed so she was using her own garden to reconstruct that day. The three of them had gone in. Mandy had trailed along reluctantly, after Petra had given her one of her withering looks. As soon as they'd got through the side gate Mandy had decided that she would be the bravest of them and walked ahead. She'd gone straight into the overgrown grass and right up the middle, past the trees and the old swing. She went to the very bottom of the garden where there were a couple of old sheds and she'd stood there feeling gratified that Tina had followed her and not stayed with Petra.

She'd been standing then as she was now with her back to the shed, looking up the garden at the rear of the house. Petra, for all her bravado, had stayed by the building and seemed to be fiddling with the ivy that grew across the brickwork. For a few moments Mandy had felt good. Tina was there with her and they had ventured much further into the old property than Petra had.

Then the neighbour had seen them and shouted.

Now Mandy looked to the left where the fence of her garden was. It was high and solid. On that day over five years ago the garden fence where the neighbour was standing had been broken, and some of it lay flat on the ground. That's why the sight of him had been such a shock. It was as if he suddenly materialised in the garden with them. They had run away like mad from him. That was all she remembered.

Her phone beeped. She took it out and saw the name 'Jon Wallis' on the screen.

Why not come round mine this evening and listen to some of my vinyls?

It was the third text he'd sent her since Friday, when they'd chatted on their way to school. He liked her, she knew. He was a nice person, easy to talk to, but he wasn't Tommy Eliot and she couldn't pretend otherwise. Even though she knew that nothing would happen between her and Tommy it didn't mean that she could just switch off her emotions. They were still there, deep down, even though she was no longer upset by them. Underneath the text from Jon was one from Lucy that'd arrived late last night:

**Mum's running a Sat course on 'Working with Silver'.
She says we can go for free if we make the tea and
tidy up afterwards. What do you think?**

She'd already replied to it saying she would go. Lucy hadn't given up trying to be friendly and Mandy had enjoyed having someone to sit with at lunchtimes. Her mum was really nice too and she loved learning about the jewellery making.

She thought about what answer to send to Jon. She had made excuses on the previous texts but it didn't seem right to keep doing it. She remembered those weeks in the first half of term when she had been drawn along by Tommy. Had he intended her to think that he cared for her? She would never know. She composed a reply.

**Sorry, Jon, I'm still too hung up on someone
else to be good company.**

She pressed 'Send' quickly so that she didn't lose her confidence.

She stared up the garden.

There was another decision she still had to make. She pulled the card Officer Farraday had given her out of her pocket. Should she tell the police officer that she'd seen Petra? She'd thought about it all weekend. The previous evening it'd come more into focus because her mum had said that Alison Pointer had just been round and told her that there had been another sighting of Tina – this time in Greece. Her mother said Alison seemed less keen to actually go herself but was in touch with a Greek organisation who were liaising with the police on her behalf. Alison had seemed tired and out of sorts, her mum had told her, and she'd been wearing jeans and an old jumper. It made Mandy feel bad.

Why shouldn't Alison know that Tina hadn't stayed in the old house; that whatever happened to Tina happened to her *on her own*?

But Mandy was still concerned that if she told the police she'd seen and spoken to Petra they might not actually believe her. And even if they took her seriously would there be some kind of blame allotted to her because she'd waited so long to tell them? It was three weeks since she'd seen Petra. Why had she waited so long? Wasn't it a kind of replay of that night in October when the girls went missing? She'd known they'd gone in the house but she'd waited five hours to tell anyone then as well. Wouldn't this just confirm how secretive she was, how she was always taking time to think of her own skin before others? In fact, wasn't that what she was doing right this minute standing in her garden?

But she had thought about other things too.

If Tina was really was dead, was there any point in ruining Petra's new life?

Mandy stared up the garden at her own house and tried to picture exactly what the back of the old house had looked like. It was much bigger than hers and much older. The only detail she could remember was that the wall was thick with ivy. There had definitely been a door. Petra had said that she and Tina went into the kitchen and that was when Tina became afraid. They must have gone through that door.

265

Mandy imagined the scene: the back door wide open and two twelve-year-old trespassers standing there. One of them wanted to go further. The other was afraid. There was tugging and whispering. It would have been pitch-dark because the old man only lived in the front part of the house. There would have been no light spilling out of windows and the garden would have been thick with bushes and overgrown foliage.

At one point Tina had decided she didn't want to go any further.

Mandy closed her eyes. It was hard to picture Tina at twelve years old but she held onto the image of a skinny girl whose hair was a bit bushy. She'd been wearing her mum's hoodie which was far too big for her. She must have stepped away from Petra and stood by the door. Had she said she was going? Had she said goodbye? Had she tried to persuade Petra to go with her?

If Petra was telling the truth then Tina turned and came out of the back door. She would have been moving quickly because she was frightened. Had she dashed along the house and turned into the pathway to the side gate? There were no lights guiding her, just blackness. Had she traced her way back round the side of the house in the inky dark? Or had she, in her confusion, turned around and run into the back garden, straight through the foliage, the long grass and past the swing? Had she run down to the end of the garden where the two of them had gone that day a couple of weeks before?

Mandy pictured Tina standing at the wall, near the sheds, confused and frightened. Had she come to a full stop and known then that she'd gone the wrong way? Had she spun around?

A terrible feeling was taking hold of Mandy.

If Tina turned round, what she might have seen? She glanced to her left and saw her own garden fence, solid and uniform, each panel fixed to the next. On that night it would have been dark and the fence would have been broken.

She tried to picture it. Tina, confused and scared. Had she seen a man standing there? Where the fence should have been? Had it made her jump? The angry neighbour would have been staring at her, his big belly sticking out, his face full of fury that she was there after he'd shouted at her last time. 'Sorry,' she might have gasped, but maybe she didn't get a chance to say any more as he took her by the arm and pulled her into his garden. Maybe he put his hand across her mouth to stop her shouting out. Or possibly he had to pick her up, her legs and arms wriggling, until he took her into his house and shut the door.

Mandy imagined the door banging and heard the key as it turned in the lock.

Then she opened her eyes as if from a bad dream. Her hands were screwed up into fists. She uncurled them and saw Officer Farraday's card crumpled in one of them. There was a sound from her house: the front door slamming. It was her mum. She *would* tell her now. She would not wait hours or days or weeks. She wouldn't keep this story to herself, even if it meant Petra's new life would be exposed. Alison had a right to know what had happened to Tina, however terrible the truth was.

The back door swung open and her mum stood there.

'What are you doing?' she called down the garden, looking a bit upset.

Mandy walked towards her, taking a deep breath, knowing what she had to say. When she got up to the door she was shaken to find her mum crying, tears rolling down her face. It was as if *she knew* what Mandy was going to tell her.

'What?' she said, holding Officer Farraday's card in her fingers. Her mum pulled a tissue out and wiped her eyes.

'I've just seen Alison in Princess Street. She's in a terrible state. The police have found Tina.'

Thirty-One

Princess Street was full of people and police cars. Mandy and her mother walked among them. They were looking for Alison Pointer. They edged through the crowd standing around and saw her in the middle of a throng. She was by a police officer and another was trying to move people away from her. There were three police cars and several officers. Two of them stood guard outside number fifty-five Princess Street. Next door the building site was at a standstill, and men in yellow hats stood around smoking cigarettes and looking serious. A truck with giant bags of sand on it was parked half up on the pavement and the driver was in a heated discussion with a WPC.

'Alison,' Mandy's mum called out.

Alison turned round and saw them. She gave a slight nod to acknowledge them but her face was frozen. Her mum edged through the people and grabbed Alison's arm. Then Alison seemed to crumple, leaning sideways on her mum's shoulder. The policeman raised his voice and people around appeared to slink away, moving back along the street. There was crime scene tape across the road and Mandy noticed a van with a satellite dish on the top beyond it.

The newsagent was outside on the pavement, his face grim, appearing to be unhappy about his street making the news again.

Mandy walked over to Alison. Her mum was holding her up now.

'He took her,' she said, looking at Mandy, her eyes glittering with tears. 'That bastard took her. My Tina's been there for the last five years.'

Mandy knew that Tina wasn't in there alive. This wasn't going to be like the girls in Cleveland, Ohio. She wasn't going to be rescued. Tina was dead, her mum had told her while walking round there. Tina's body was probably buried in the cellar of the house and the police intended to find it. Alison knew these things but she had talked about Tina as if she were alive for the last five years and it was hard for her to say it any other way.

Mandy looked at the house that she'd seen the neighbour come out of days before. It was an old end-of-terrace building and the front garden had been paved. There were no flowers there in contrast to other gardens along the way. Its curtains were drawn top and bottom. The police officers standing at the gate had no expressions on their faces. The front door opened unexpectedly, silencing the small crowd. Two men in white paper suits came out. They were carrying items inside thick plastic bags. One of them looked bulky. It was a computer screen, cumbersome and heavy; it looked as if it had been bought many years before.

'Mrs Pointer?' a woman said.

Alison turned around. A woman in a dark quilted jacket stood there.

'Detective Constable Bernice Morgan. I think it would be a good idea if we retired to your home. That way I can keep you up to date with the search. Maybe your friends could come and make you something to eat.'

'I don't want to eat.'

Alison was staring at the house, her forehead lined, her teeth gritted.

'That would be a good idea,' her mum said, pulling her gently away. 'Let's go. It's just a couple of streets. We can walk.'

'Best to go in my car,' DC Morgan said. 'The press will be everywhere.'

'I can deal with the press,' Alison said.

'We know you can but now isn't the time,' her mum said.

Alison nodded. She let go of Mandy's mum's arm and began to walk. The DC took her elbow and led her through the onlookers. They knew who she was. They stood back respectfully. Mandy looked back at the house.

'Is he in custody?' she said.

Her mum frowned.

'The man who lives there. Have the police got him?'

Her mum linked Mandy's arm and drew her away.

'Oh, Mandy, he killed himself. They think he did it Friday night. He posted a letter to the police confessing what happened and an officer went there this morning. They found him dead.'

'Oh.'

She'd seen the angry neighbour twice on Friday. She'd passed him as he got out of a cab on Friday evening.

They were heading for the DC's car. Alison was already in the passenger seat.

'How did he do it?' Mandy said.

'He took sleeping tablets. He had bottles of them apparently. Maybe he'd been planning it for years and the demolition of the house was a trigger.'

It was the first time that Mandy had been inside Alison's home since she'd been friends with Tina. It had changed a lot. Then it had been wooden floors and lots of pictures and decorative ornaments. There'd been rugs here and there and scatter cushions on every available seat. There had always been things to look at, little mementoes that the family had brought back from somewhere. In those days it hadn't always been a happy place because Tina's mum was upset about her husband who was no longer living there. Now it was clean and neat with oatmeal carpets on the floors and a beige sofa with black throws over the arms and back. There were no small things on view. It was an emotionless place, like a waiting room.

Mandy's mum dashed off to the kitchen, calling, 'I'll see what's in the fridge.' Mandy hoped she wasn't planning to bake anything. Alison sat in the middle of the sofa with her hands sandwiched between her legs. She stared straight ahead. DC Morgan was beside her. Mandy perched on the armchair opposite. Her mum came out of the kitchen.

'Shall I make some toast? There's not much else. I could pop out to the shops? There's some tins of soup . . .'

She was talking quickly with an air of panic in her voice.

'Perhaps we could just have some tea for Alison,' DC Morgan said. 'That would be a start. I would like a cup of tea and I'm sure Mandy would too.'

Her mum went off. Mandy was disconcerted that the detective knew her name, but of course she would. Mandy was no bit player in this. She was at the heart of it. No one said anything while the tea was being made. Her mum brought it in and handed the mugs around. Alison put hers straight on the carpet by her foot. DC Morgan spoke quietly and without any sense of drama.

'The things I'm going to explain will be in the public domain any minute now: television, radio, social media. So you need to know what is going on. On Saturday a letter was delivered to Holloway Road Police Station. It wasn't addressed to any particular person so it was channelled through admin. The letter was not opened until this morning. It was a confession: two pages of closely written text. As soon as it had been read, officers went to the address. They had to break down the door of the house and Alan Monk was found dead on his bed. Beside him were a couple of hairslides. We believe these may have belonged to Tina.'

Alison made an audible gasp.

DC Morgan stopped. Her face took on a look of shame as if it were her fault in some way. The neighbour's name was Alan Monk. Mandy realised then that she'd only ever thought of him as the *angry neighbour*.

'I thought you checked all the houses. And the Sex Offender Register,' her mum said.

'We did check the register. There were a couple of men who lived in the area at the time and their homes were searched and they were questioned. But Alan Monk had no record. He'd never been known to the police.'

DC Morgan turned to Alison and grabbed her hand.

'Alison,' she said, 'the confession does not suggest that there was a sexual motive although we can't know that for sure until we find Tina. And of course we are checking Alan Monk's computer, his associates, his life.'

The detective spoke about finding *Tina*, not finding a body.

'Is she definitely dead?' Mandy blurted out.

'I'm afraid so. The confession states this and has told us where to find the body.'

'It could be made up,' Alison said, sitting up straight, an energy coming from her. 'This man could be a fantasist. He's lived next door to it all these years and he could have persuaded himself . . .'

'He has her clothes, Alison. There are signs that the floor in the cellar has been disturbed. We are excavating now. We will know soon.'

Alison shook her head. 'I don't believe it. Not after all these years. There was no body. I've always known that she was alive. I've felt it here.'

She had her hand over her chest; her fingers were thin and fragile like an old lady's.

'And anyway,' Alison went on, 'what does the letter say about Petra? Petra isn't mentioned. And they were together. I always knew they'd be together, they'd look after each other. I always knew that Petra would look after my Tina.'

This wasn't true. There were many times that Alison had come round to their house and talked about sightings of Tina *on her own*. She had not mentioned Petra then.

A mobile ringtone sounded. It made them all look round sharply. DC Morgan answered her phone. Mandy's mum got

274

up and sat next to Alison. She put her arm round her. Mandy could hear the DC saying, 'Yes . . . Yes, I'll do that . . . I'll tell her . . . Yes . . .' The call ended. DC Morgan paused before she spoke.

'Alison, I'm sorry to tell you but our officers have found a body under the cellar of Alan Monk's house. It's the body of a female approximately twelve years old. We'll know more later, after the autopsy.'

Alison seemed to steel herself. Mandy wondered if she was going to cry. She didn't though. She disengaged herself from Mandy's mum and stood up.

'I need to get changed,' she said. 'I need to get myself ready.'

Mandy avoided making eye contact with her and looked away, around the room. Over by the door she saw Alison's handbag, solid and square, sitting on the carpet. She wondered if it was full of the things Alison needed, ready to go to any possible sightings of Tina. Would she take it with her now? For what? To identify her daughter's clothes?

'Could Petra be there as well?' Mandy's mum said. 'In that cellar?'

'No. At the present moment we don't believe that Petra is part of this and we have no idea what happened to her.'

They all looked at Mandy. They had sympathy in their eyes because Mandy had been Petra's friend and was closer to her than any of them. They didn't know that Mandy had seen and spoken to Petra already. They didn't know what Mandy knew.

PART SIX: The Present

Klara

Thirty-Two

Klara stared out of her bedroom window onto the street below. It had stopped snowing and there were people walking along the pavement. They were wearing their great coats, boots and woollen hats, and a couple of old ladies had scarves covering their noses and mouths. Some cars were driving slowly down the road, one of them skidding a little, then righting itself.

The house was warm, the radiators piping hot. She could hear a clanking sound from the radiator in the bathroom which Henryk was always trying to fix.

Klara was glad to be on her own. Zofia and Henryk had gone out for some DIY shopping because Henryk wanted to redecorate the kitchen. Henryk was never happy with rooms until he had stripped them back and changed them around. He planned a breakfast bar for the kitchen. Zofia liked the idea and they'd decided to start next week. He'd asked Klara to come and help but she'd said no. 'You got boyfriend coming?' he'd said to her in English.

Zofia had given him a slap on the head and told him, in Polish, that Klara was too young for boys. Henryk liked to speak the odd bit of English. 'Keep in excellent practice,' he'd say.

Klara did have a boyfriend, but it was a secret from Zofia who worried about her all the time. 'Boys just want one thing,' she'd whisper in English. When they were on their own Zofia often spoke to Klara in English but everywhere else it was Polish.

Her boyfriend was the son of a friend of Marya's. His name was Pawel and he supported Manchester United. He liked comic book heroes and collected old-magazines about them which he shopped for on the web. He had brown hair that was cut short and Klara liked to run her fingers through it. He liked to play with her hair as well, teasing it out of the grips she wore. He liked to undo her buttons too but she always stopped him, because she knew how upset Zofia would be if anything happened. Neither Henryk nor Zofia knew about Pawel but Klara suspected that Marya had a good idea what was going on. But Marya wouldn't give her secret away.

Her phone beeped and she took it out of her pocket. It was a text from Pawel.

Tęsknię za tobą. XXX

He missed her. He'd only seen her a couple of nights ago. She smiled and tapped out a quick reply because, actually, she missed him too.

Za tobą tęsknię ☺

She kept her phone out as she sat looking down into the street. She was playing with the cross that hung on the chain around her neck. She held it up to her lips and felt the cold metal. Once it had belonged to Klara, Zofia's real sister. Zofia had given it to her as a gift and she wore it always. Zofia had given her many gifts over the years and Henryk was generous too. Her room was full of CDs and DVD sets, books and gadgets.

The window felt cold but she stayed there anyway. She could see all the way down the road and there was a crocodile of very young schoolchildren being led along by their teachers. They were each wearing a lime green tabard over their coat. They all had woollen hats and gloves and they were walking in twos, holding hands. They were so small that the snow was nearly up to their knees.

Klara was starting a new college after Christmas. After spending much of the autumn in Paris and London, picking up work here and there, they had returned to Lodz a couple of weeks before Christmas and it hadn't been worth Klara going to college for that short time. She didn't mind. She liked being at home with Zofia and Henryk.

She hadn't had long periods of schooling. The first year after she left London she didn't go to school at all. They moved around Poland. For a few months they stayed near Krakow in Henryk's flat while he and his van did different trips back and forth across the continent. Then they moved north and Henryk came with them. He stopped taking long trips and started up a cab business. They spent a couple of years near the Ukrainian border and Klara went to a school there for a while. By then her Polish was fluent. Then they went to Gdansk, a port on the Baltic Sea, which Klara thought was the coldest place on earth. There she dressed up to go bed with socks, leg warmers, pyjamas and a night cap. Zofia was happy though, and didn't seem to notice the ice-laden winds and the freezing sunshine.

Klara knew why Zofia was moving round. She couldn't stay in one place in case her father came after them. Henryk knew who Klara really was, although she didn't know what explanation Zofia had given him.

They finally ended up in Lotz, the place where Marya had her nail shop. Marya found a house for them and they settled, except there wasn't much work. Henryk decided to become a man with a van in London again for a while, so Zofia said she should go with him and Klara could stay with Marya. But Klara wouldn't be separated from Zofia. Klara went back to London with Zofia and Henryk and they worked at a variety of jobs to get money to bring back to Poland.

Early one morning, on the way to a bakery they were working at, Klara said, 'Why don't we just drive past the old house?' Princess Street was on their way, so Zofia didn't mind. They stopped at the house, except it wasn't there any more. It had been flattened and she got out to look at it. Then *there* was Mandy Crystal, all grown up, standing in the shadows, talking to her like a ghost.

She had never been as frightened as she had been at that moment. (Actually, she had, when her father had *killed a man*.) Everything she had gained over the past five years seemed to be in jeopardy, just because she'd stepped out of a car and stood in front of a fence. How close she had been to losing her new life. Even when Mandy had turned up on her doorstep she hadn't been so scared. Because Mandy hadn't gone to the police straight away. Mandy just wanted to know what had happened and Klara was able to give her a version of the truth.

Out in the street in Lotz, below her window, she could see Henryk's car coming along. Now he would moan because there was nowhere for him to park. She watched it go by and knew that he would have things in the back to carry along to the house. She pulled her boots out from under her bed and slipped her feet into the fur-lined interiors. She laced them up and looked round for her jumper. Even going out for a few minutes she had to make sure she was warm enough. She went downstairs, pulled her coat out of the cupboard by the radiator and then looked for her gloves.

Zofia had shown her the news reports about the police finding the body of Tina Pointer under the cellar of the neighbour's house. It had surprised her because Zofia never talked about those days in Holloway when she worked in a nail shop and was the girlfriend of Jason Armstrong, Klara's father. Klara had always assumed that Zofia had almost forgotten that bit of her life, that perhaps she had begun to believe that Klara really was her sister.

But a week ago she had waited until Henryk went out and pulled Klara over to look at her laptop. There it was, the whole story. The body of one of the two Moth Girls had been found. The disappearance of the second girl, Petra Armstrong, was still a mystery and the police would continue to investigate. Klara had cried for Tina but not for long. She had tried her hardest to go back to that night and in her imagination follow Tina out into the garden as she ran away from the old house. But it was as if those memories belonged to someone else. Klara couldn't make herself concentrate on them. The girl Petra had gone and now she was someone different.

She did her coat up and pulled on her hat. She opened the door and felt the force of the wind and some speckles of snow that were blowing from nearby drifts. She made sure she had her door key and looked up and down the white street. Trundling along from the far corner was Henryk, carrying bags in each hand. Zofia was beside him with rolls of something under her arm. They must have parked round by the tyre workshop where there were always places. Klara walked swiftly towards them and when they met Henryk's face lit up.

'*Moja mała róża,*' he said.

My little rose.

'*Jest tak zimno. Zrobię zupę dla ciebie,*' Klara said.

She'd make some soup for them.

'*Dzięki,*' Zofia said, grabbing her collar and pulling her face down so that she could give her a big kiss on the cheek.

Klara was much taller than her sister. Some people thought this was odd but Zofia just laughed it off and told them that *everyone* was taller than her.

Her phone beeped. She glanced down at it. It was Pawel. Another text!

'Boyfriend,' Henryk said in English.

Klara didn't answer. She took one of the bags off him and trekked back through the snow towards the house.

She'd answer it later. When she'd made the soup for Zofia and Henryk.

Anne Cassidy

Anne Cassidy was born in London in 1952. She was an awkward teenager who spent the Swinging Sixties stuck in a convent school trying, dismally, to learn Latin. She was always falling in love and having her heart broken. She worked in a bank for five years until she finally grew up. She then went to college before becoming a teacher for many years. In 2000 Anne became a full-time writer, specialising in crime stories and thrillers for teenagers. In 2004 LOOKING FOR JJ was published to great acclaim, going on to be shortlisted for the 2004 Whitbread Prize and the 2005 Carnegie Medal. Follow Anne at www.annecassidy.com or on Twitter: @annecassidy6

HOT KEY BOOKS

Thank you for choosing a Hot Key book.

If you want to know more about our authors and what we publish, you can find us online.

You can start at our website

www.hotkeybooks.com

And you can also find us on:

We hope to see you soon!